FEMALE(S AND)
DOGS

Spineless Wonders
ABN98156041888
PO Box 220 STRAWBERRY HILLS
New South Wales, Australia, 2012
www.shortaustralianstories.com.au

First published by Spineless Wonders 2020

Typeset in Adobe Garamond Pro

National Library of Australia
Female(s and) Dogs /Brooke Dunnell
ISBN 978-1-925052-63-3

A823.4

A catalogue record for this book is available from the National Library of Australia

This project has been assisted by the Copyright Agency Cultural Fund.

FEMALE(S AND) DOGS

BROOKE DUNNELL

CONTENTS

The Mistress

Faye watches the car loop the block three times before pulling up at the end of her driveway and idling there. She counts out thirty seconds and then steps outside, shutting the dogs in the house.

The driver of the car kills the engine and emerges holding up a hand in peace. 'Faye Hagan?' he calls.

'Don't stand around shouting in the road,' she says.

'I'm sorry?'

She shakes her head and he walks up the long driveway. His footsteps crunch. He stops a few feet away.

'Miss Hagan?'

'What's this about?' she asks, eyeing his phone. He's holding it out in front of him, the screen angled like a suncatcher.

'I'm Oliver Keate, a reporter with Siren Call Media. I'm—'

'With who?'

'Siren Call.'

'Never heard of them.'

He straightens his shoulders. 'I'm doing a podcast about the disappearance of Lorna McGuire.'

Faye's sigh is a white wisp, gone in a moment. Twenty-four years is nothing, it turns out. Twenty-four years is a breath in the wind.

The young man looks past her. He has shaggy hair and freckles and could be her son. He wouldn't have been born when Lorna went missing.

'I was hoping we could talk,' he says.

'I was interviewed three times by police,' Faye tells him. 'My story's out there.'

'We want to look at things with fresh eyes. See if anything was missed.'

'You're a detective, then?' She crosses her arms. 'I thought you were a reporter.'

'Renewed interest in the case could help solve it, don't you think?' Oliver tips his chin towards the house and smiles. 'Do you have time to chat?'

Rosie and Zeus jump at the visitor in the entryway, sniffing the fresh smells and butting their dumb skulls at his phone. Holding the device out of the way, he drops to a knee and scratches each dog behind the ear with his free hand. 'Gorgeous. Maltese terriers, am I right? Do you breed them?'

He's recording everything, Faye realises. 'They breed when they want to. It's not a full-time operation.'

Penned in the corner, a third dog, Dido, whines and scrabbles at the floor.

Oliver looks around at Faye. 'Does she not like humans?'

'She loves humans. It's other bitches she can't get along with.'

The podcaster flinches at the word. 'I suppose even animals get jealous.'

'She shouldn't be. Rosie was here first. If anyone's the mistress, it's Dido.'

Oliver stands and slides his hand between the plastic bars of Dido's pen. Delighted, the dog rises on her back legs, displaying rubbery grey nipples.

'She's had puppies,' he comments.

'Yes,' Faye says, shortly. 'Would you like a cup of tea?'

In the kitchen she switches on the kettle and assembles a plate of broken Arrowroots. Her daughter listens to these true crime podcasts. When they drove out to Wally Ridge at Christmas, she'd played one about a girl who crashed her car in snowy weather and vanished, never to be seen again. It made Faye's teeth throb.

Tragedy is not entertainment. When she had a chance to change the soundtrack, she put on John Farnham's *Best Of* and let her daughter sulk.

Oliver has taken a seat on the couch and set his phone on the coffee table. Rosie is stretched out beside him and Zeus lies at his feet. Traitors, both of them.

Faye sits in her chair. 'Aren't you meant to ask before putting me on tape?'

Oliver reaches for a mug of tea. 'Do you consent to being recorded?'

'What's the show called?'

'*Missing Lorna*,' he says. Faye rolls her eyes. 'So are you giving your consent?'

She bites into an Arrowroot and makes him wait while she chews. 'Suppose I'll have to.' She sighs, sitting back against the cushions.

'Very much appreciated. We just want to shed some light on this mystery.'

Dido yelps from the corner. Faye hates to leave her there, but she's still leaking milk and biting Rosie if she goes near Zeus.

Shaking her head, Faye takes another biscuit. Mouth full, she mumbles, 'What's your angle? The boyfriend did it?'

It was the most popular theory. Kenny Benoit had been spitting drunk, and furious when Lorna wouldn't leave the party with him.

He had made a scene in front of everyone and chased her down the road. He had a gun in the boot of his car. The Benoits had hired a lawyer by the end of the first day.

'He's a good suspect,' Oliver says.

'They cleared him. No evidence.'

'He lit a fire in his vehicle.'

'He didn't *light*...' Faye begins, irritable, then sees the unblinking black eye of the phone. 'It was a dropped cigarette. He was sitting out there, thinking about her.'

'Sitting in the back seat of your own car,' the podcaster comments. 'It's unusual, wouldn't you say?'

Faye shrugs.

Oliver leans forward and prods the phone another inch in her direction as she asks, 'That guy confessed, didn't he?'

Oliver names the career criminal who'd laid claim in prison to kidnapping Lorna. 'The police say he's a fantasist, an attention seeker.

He takes credit for crimes he had nothing to do with.'

'But he must've done some of them.'

'There's no evidence he was ever in Wally Ridge.'

'He was nearby,' Faye argues, then adds, 'I thought I heard.'

'He would've had to be on that road at the exact right time.

There were only minutes in it. Seconds.'

Sleuths love a timeline, Faye has learned. There was one during the podcast her daughter had played: a moment-by-moment countdown until the girl disappeared. Most important to Lorna's case are the seconds after Kenny stormed out of the party and down the street after her. He says he caught up with her at the next corner but she refused a lift. Her house was close and she was going to walk. That was the last time anyone ever saw her.

Faye shakes her head.

'Something on your mind?' Oliver asks.

'I wasn't at the party,' Faye says. 'Some of the papers said I was, but my parents wouldn't let me go. They didn't want me drinking.'

'It must have felt awful when you found out what happened.'

Faye allows this comment to pass unacknowledged.

Oliver leans down and scratches Zeus, making him twitch joyously against the rug. 'Good boy,' he croons. 'What a good boy.'

The sight of Zeus's abjection makes Faye cringe. She wants to call the dog over to her, make him behave. 'I don't know what else to tell you,' she says.

Oliver straightens. 'You helped to search the next day, right?'

His tone is smooth and reminds her of the psychologists she's talked to over the years. She tells herself that it doesn't matter what he sounds like. There's no confidentiality here: Oliver wants to squeeze whatever he can out of her every word.

'What was that like?'

Her head had rung like a bell as they shuffled in lines through the bush, scanning the ground and calling her friend's name. At the party, Lorna had been wearing a short, purple jumper, which should have been easy to spot among all the green and brown.

Kenny was being interviewed down at the station. 'Stressful,' she says honestly. 'I wanted to find my friend.'

'Kenny Benoit says,' Oliver begins, then pauses to pick up his phone and swipe through several screens. Nodding, he puts it back. 'He says that when she refused his offer of a lift, he drove down to the river instead. He sat there for a while to sober up, then went home. His mother said he came in at half past one.'

Faye sees ripples forming on the surface of her tea.

'Two hours after Lorna left the party,' Oliver adds.

Faye clicks her shaky fingers and Zeus stands up, groggy. He staggers a few steps in her direction and slumps back down.

'They used sniffer dogs,' the young man continues. 'Lorna's scent was tracked from the party location approximately seven hundred metres down the road. It would've taken her five or six minutes to walk that distance, if she was in a hurry. As it's assumed she was.'

Faye drinks down her tea.

'She was heading in the direction of the river,' he says. 'Exactly where Kenny ended up.'

'I know all this.'

'What else do you know?'

Faye holds his gaze. If this little smart-arse thinks he's going to get something out of her that the police couldn't, he's deluding himself. 'They dragged the river. She wasn't in it.'

Oliver's smile doesn't reach his eyes. 'Something I might not know already. To complete the picture.'

'I can't tell you anything about the party. I didn't go.'

'Anything in general. Anything could help.'

'She was a very kind person,' Faye answers sincerely. She imagines her words in the ears of people like her daughter and tries to speak towards the phone. 'Full of love and life.'

'She deserves justice,' he summarises.

Faye's skin prickles. She turns to check on Dido, who has lain down on her towel and gone to sleep.

'How did she feel about Kenny?' Oliver asks.

'He was her boyfriend.'

'Did he treat her well?'

'Supposedly he was having a go at her, like you said. About wanting to have sex.' She swallows. 'But he didn't hit her or anything. She never told me he did.'

'Did he seem violent to you?'

'I didn't know him very well,' Faye says. 'I only met him a few times.' This is the truth. It's all the truth.

'But you don't think he did it.'

'I think there would've been evidence.'

'Do you find it bizarre,' Oliver begins, 'that he would go and sit in his car for two hours in the middle of the night?'

'I don't know.'

'And then have a smoke in the back seat the next day?'

Faye lifts her mug and finds it empty. 'I didn't know him very well,' she repeats.

'How was your relationship with Lorna?'

'We'd been best friends a long time.'

She gets up and clears away the plates. There's still some tea in Oliver's cup. When she comes back from the kitchen she doesn't sit down, hoping he'll take the hint. He's flipping through his phone again, looking comfortable.

'I'm busy now,' she says.

Before he leaves, Oliver goes over to the pen and leans down to farewell Dido, who rolls onto her back, teats erect like bolts along her belly. Oliver scratches her side. 'How many puppies did she have?'

'Two.'

'Sold already?' He digs deeply into the dog's ribs. 'They can't have been old.'

'She lost them both,' Faye murmurs. 'They weren't well.' 'Jesus.' Oliver looks genuinely upset. His pats soften. 'Sorry, girl. Sorry.'

He walks to the door slowly, lingering, trying to get her to say something else. Faye is patient. She raised a daughter through to adulthood. She knows how to wait things out.

When Oliver has gone, Faye lifts Dido from her pen and carries her onto the back patio, shutting the other dogs inside the house.

She settles on an old deck chair with Dido on her lap and looks out to the bush beyond. She lives far from Wally Ridge now, so this is nowhere near where Lorna disappeared, but the landscape is similar. Sometimes she sees a flash of purple among the trees.

Faye was very careful to be honest with Oliver. She'd been the same with the police, all three times. She did not attend the house party. She doesn't know what happened to Lorna. She didn't really know Kenny, but she's always been certain he was innocent.

The cops hadn't liked hearing that.

Scratching comes from the back door: Rosie and Zeus, wanting to come out. She shouts at them to go away. This time is just for poor Dido, penned up all day, haunted by jealousy and the loss of her pups. A square of sun slides over them and Faye closes her eyes.

She hasn't lied, but that doesn't mean she has no regrets. She's full of them, crippled by them, her daughter would say. She'd been kind but frustrated when Faye had a panic attack driving to Wally Ridge and demanded she turn off the podcast. 'It's just a story,' her daughter said, pulling her auxiliary cable from the dashboard. 'You always take everything so personally.'

The girl on the podcast had stepped beyond the tree line and vanished. A killer might have found her in that tiny window of time, but it was the middle of the night, the temperature below freezing, and she most likely died of exposure. They searched for her many times, but nature is big, and bodies are small. A scared young woman might curl up beneath a fallen branch and wink into another world, like Alice in Wonderland.

Other people, including Faye's daughter, believe the podcast girl stepped out of her life and into another. A new identity, a new country. There's hope in that. No-one wants to think of a frightened young person dying lost and alone, or, worse, hurt by some stranger. Better to imagine they stepped through the looking glass.

Faye wouldn't say to anyone, because it sounds ridiculous, but this is what she thinks happened that night. It wasn't the boyfriend or the boastful criminal: it was Lorna, shedding the sadness and stress of her old life and sliding into a new one. Three kilometres from the party house, after you cross the river, there'd been a highway full of truckies who didn't ask hitchhikers any questions.

Still, Faye thinks. Still.

Dido jumps down from her lap and staggers into the bush, but Faye barely notices. Her version is blurry from twenty-four years away.

She'd been coming up the street when Lorna ran out in that stomach-bearing top, stalactites of mascara in her eyes. Seeing Faye arrive, Lorna flailed her arms, crying loudly, and Faye felt a small flash of revulsion. To Lorna, every little thing was the end of the world.

Faye had stroked Lorna's hair while she sobbed about Kenny.

He'd called her a tease, Lorna moaned, and Faye looked at her thick makeup and bare white belly and wondered what it was, really, that Lorna expected.

Kenny came out soon after, just as the story said. Spotting them from the verandah, he stumbled down the steps and over the front lawn, half-chasing the girls as Lorna tried to pull Faye back the way she'd come. There were no houses at this end of the road, only thickening scrub. Faye watched the bright lights of the party house recede as she trailed behind Lorna. 'Let's go back,' she begged, but Lorna had only whimpered and stumbled along the bitumen. Not caring what Faye wanted, as usual.

Catching up to them, Kenny tried to take his girl-friend's hand. Lorna tugged herself free and hooked her finger through Faye's belt-loop, using her as an anchor. 'No!' she said. 'Leave me alone.' The small tides of disgust built to a wave inside Faye. She'd slid out the side window of her parents' house to have a good time, not to deal with this bullshit.

Kenny was apologising, but Lorna wouldn't hear it.

'Fine,' he said eventually. 'Walk home. I'm leaving.'

His car was a bit further down, parked on the soft shoulder near the turn-off to Faye's street. He stalked off towards it, keys jangling. Uncertain, the two girls hovered where they were, Lorna dragging on Faye like a dead weight.

Kenny stopped by the driver's side door. 'One last chance.'

Lorna shook her head. Releasing her grip on Faye, she lifted the neck of her jumper and bit the fabric.

Free, Faye heard herself say, 'I'll come.'

Kenny stared for a moment, trying to work out what she meant. Faye stepped away from Lorna, who whined her name. Heading for the car, Faye had tried to act like this all came naturally to her. Kenny went to open the passenger door and she looked up at the stars.

They got in and drove to the river. For a while they'd been on the back seat, and when they finished Kenny dropped Faye at the end of her road. His mother said he got home at 1:32 am. Mrs Benoit was up reading. Her son looked a little rumpled and his cheeks were flushed, she reported, but there was no blood or dirt on him. He went straight to bed.

Instead of going home, Faye had traced her steps back to the party. The windows of the once-buzzing house were dark. In the yard, empty cans shone in the moonlight. Returning to the end of her street, Faye saw the tyre tracks in the dirt where she and Kenny had left Lorna. She wanted to call out into the bush for her, but that was dumb: Lorna would have long since been home by then. Numbed, Faye walked the rest of the way to her own quiet house, sliding back through the open window without waking her parents.

Two days later someone said Kenny was home from the police station, so she went to the Benoits' and waited by the letterbox until she saw him come out. Again, they drove to the river and got in the back seat. When they were done Kenny took a cigarette from the glovebox. 'If they decide to search the car,' Kenny said, flicking his lighter, 'they might find traces of you.'

'I'll tell them everything,' she said. 'I know you didn't do it.'

'People would kill you,' Kenny said.

Her gut lurched at the word.

He passed over the cigarette. 'I'm serious.'

'I can handle it.' She sucked lightly and coughed.

He looked at her. 'No, you can't.'

She gave him back the cigarette and he drew smoke deep into his lungs.

'You don't have to say anything,' Kenny had said. Emotion thickened his words. 'It's none of their business anyway. I told them the truth. She wouldn't go with me, so I went to the river, then I went home.'

'Are you sure?'

'I didn't do anything,' Kenny said. 'But I think someone else did.'

'No,' she shouted. His eyebrows went up. 'I bet she made a run for it.'

Kenny shrugged and gave her the cigarette. She sucked on it shallowly and tried to tap out the ash in a sexy way but dropped the whole thing on the upholstery.

'Shit,' Kenny said, reaching for it and touching the tip by mistake. 'Shit, ow.' He took his hands back and sucked his fingers.

Faye watched as the cigarette rolled sideways underneath the clump of tissues Kenny had just used. After a moment's pause a brown mark appeared and spread, the tissue paper thinning and crumpling into a dirty flower, smoke curling from its charred petals. When the small conflagration had burned itself out,

Kenny flicked the tight black ball and it disintegrated, revealing a scorch mark on the polyester below.

The square of sun is long gone. Standing on stiff legs, Faye calls for Dido and heads back inside. Rosie and Zeus are asleep side by side on the lounge, drawing on each other's warmth. Instead of joining them, Dido goes over to the pen and waits for Faye to open the gate before curling up on her milk-damp towel. This had been her first whelping – Rosie has had two sets already – and it was a shit-show from the start. When the puppies died Faye had buried them out in the bush. When Dido disappears into the scrub she is visiting her dead babies. She never wanted to go out there before.

By the time Faye realised she was pregnant she hadn't spoken to Kenny in weeks. The stories had grown so crazy she'd become too afraid to tell him, even though she knew he was innocent.

She imagined him shooting her in the belly and burying her in the bush. It was what they said he'd done to Lorna. Instead, she'd waited until just before she got big enough to be noticed and moved down here to have her daughter. Faye had hoped this would be the start of her escape, but it turned out to be the sum of it.

She gets down onto the floor of the pen and curls up behind Dido, resting her head on the rancid towel. She strokes the dog's soft head and hears her sigh.

Faye imagines Lorna still out there. Bush woman, living in the hollow of a log, washing out her cropped jumper in the wide river. Twigs and leaves entwine in her long hair. She smells of eucalyptus and pollen and chews on gumnuts. She watches from her place in the trees.

Bella

The man stood on their covered verandah out of the weather, hands pushed deep into the pockets of his puffy coat, his neck shrunk into the collar. Millie kept the security door closed between them, her white legs pimpling in the cold air that came through the mesh.

'Hello?' The darkness made it difficult to see his face.

'My mate said you guys're homing some puppies.'

'Oh.' Millie looked behind her, though she knew Carolyn had gone to pick up her father from the station. 'We—'

'This the right house?' the guy interrupted. He leaned forward to try and see down the hallway. 'You guys have puppies, right?'

'My dog had puppies,' Millie said.

'My mate works with your mum. Carol, right?'

It was her stepmum, and her name was Carolyn, but Millie didn't want to correct him. She reached for the door handle, saying, 'They're not ready to go yet.'

'But I could get a preview.'

'What's your name?' she asked, as if he could give her some kind of password. Carolyn hadn't said anyone would be coming, but she didn't always remember things like that, or think it was necessary for Millie to know them.

'Jem.'

She had to let him in now. Jem paused in the doorway to shake the moisture from his coat, then slid out of it as if she'd invited him to and draped it over her own on the nearby rack. His face was pale, with a small circle of beard and curly hair wet from the rain.

'Just got off work,' he told her.

'Oh, cool,' Millie said, knowing she should be interested when people talked about themselves.

'I heard you've got some nice puppies.' His lips spread into a long smile, two hooks at each end.

Crossing her arms into her stomach, Millie turned and led him through the house. 'Bella's our Lab,' she explained. 'She only had the pups, like, three weeks ago. They're mixes, though. We're not really sure who she—'

Pausing outside the laundry door, she felt something brush against her thigh, just above the crease of her knee.

Jem said, 'Sorry. You stopped kind of suddenly.'

'Sure,' she said immediately. 'That's okay.'

Bella lay on a blanket on the laundry floor, her white stomach exposed with its rows of grey teats. Facing her was the old box containing her litter, one side ripped down so the cardboard lay flat on the tiles, a warm bridge to Bella. The pups crawled over one another like insects in a jar, and Millie bent to pick up one as it delivered needly bites along the spine of its sibling. 'Naughty!' she chided, tucking the mutt under her chin and feeling its buzzing warmth.

'Nice.' Jem stepped closer. 'I like a naughty girl.'

Millie frowned and checked underneath the puppy, but it was a boy. She crouched to release him and waited on her haunches to spot one of the girls. There were only two in the litter and Carolyn had mentioned keeping one as company for Bella.

'Is that…' Trailing off, Jem reached for a yellow pup lying on its belly. 'Think this one's a girl,' he said, tipping it upside-down over Millie's head. On the floor Bella's muzzle wrinkled, her chest popping with pre-grunts.

Millie's stomach rolled at the treatment of the dog, which was squeaking and waving its forepaws. 'That one's a boy, too,' she said, lifting her hands towards him. 'We're not supposed to handle them too much. They need to rely on Bella, not us.'

Jem shrugged. Millie returned the pup to the box and stood up with her pelvis tucked, aware of how short her school skirt could be.

They stood in silence, Jem with his hands on his hips, moons of sweat in the pits of his shirt. Millie put one toe to her opposite heel and twisted her calf, feeling static in her chest and shoulders. Rain washed down the louvered windows.

'Do you want a cup of tea?' she asked, unsettled by the way he kept staring at the puppies, like choosing off a menu. 'Before you go.'

'Love a beer,' he said, looking away at last. Condensation threaded through his heavy brows. 'That'd be ace.'

Relieved, Millie shut the dogs safe in the laundry and led Jem into the kitchen. He leaned against the counter while she checked the fridge, heart falling when she saw there were only two stubbies left. Her dad would want those when he got home.

'Sorry,' she said, blocking the contents from his view. 'We don't have any.'

Jem's brow wrinkled. 'But you offered.'

'Sorry,' she repeated. 'I can get you a glass of water?'

'Anything harder?' When she bit her lip, confused, he explained, 'Y'know, whisky, bourbon, something like that. Rum.'

'Oh.' Millie feinted towards the lounge room. 'Um, how do you have it?'

Again, the thin frog smile. 'Just how it comes. Neat.'

He followed too closely, the warmth of him shadowing her neck and back, his heavy footsteps almost catching her heels. In the front room she opened her father's drinks cabinet, took out an opened bottle of Jack Daniels and poured half a glass. Jem's eyes lit up.

'Cute *and* generous, eh!' he appraised, taking a mouthful. 'Mmm,' he gargled. 'Keeps you warm, that.'

'Did you drive here?'

'Rode my pushbike.'

Millie nodded, not knowing what to say next. Jem ambled across the room and fell into her dad's armchair with his legs spread. Despite the cold weather he wore shorts made of heavy denim that rode up to show his hairy thighs. Millie waited on the other side of the room. She thought she could hear the rumbles and cries of the puppies, unless it was feedback in her ears.

'Your friend who works with Carolyn,' Millie said, 'what's he do?'

'Zac? He's a butcher.' Jem burped lightly. 'Said your mum's the nicest in the back office.'

She nodded.

'Most of 'em are old bitches. No offence.' He drained his glass. 'Great starter. Another? You should have one.'

She took the empty glass carefully, like handling evidence, and half-filled it again. The serving size was an uneducated guess: Carolyn and her father didn't drink hard liquor in front of her.

Jem nodded his receipt and took a long sip. 'Ooh, that's hit the spot.'

She made sure not to sit down, hoping to send a message, but he seemed to have settled in. 'There was no sign of Carolyn's car in the driveway. Millie hugged herself, sliding her arms up the opposite sleeves, winding herself into a knot.

Jem noticed. 'Hey, relax.' His eyebrows lifted. 'What're you so afraid of?'

Millie gave a weak smile. She disassembled the straightjacket and shook her sleeves back down.

He held out his drink. 'This'll warm you up.'

'No, thank you.'

'How old are ya?' he asked. 'Seventeen, right? Sixteen?'

Usually Millie would allow a person to believe that, but something steady inside her suggested she round down. 'Thirteen,' she lied. She'd be fifteen next week.

'Fuck,' he said in disbelief, like he'd just spotted a fin on the horizon. 'No fucken way.'

Lights pierced the front window and flashed across them. The visitor craned over the back of the chair. 'Who's that?'

'My stepmother.' Relief made Millie feel light. She smiled brightly, like a child.

He stood up, shoving the dirty glass at her. 'I'd better go.'

Jem was still pulling on his coat when Carolyn hurried inside, hands protecting her hair. The flywire crashed shut behind her.

'Whose bike is that? Mill?' she called, then stopped, seeing them both.

'This is Jem,' Millie explained. 'He wanted a look at the puppies.'

'Not really interested, thanks,' Jem said, flicking up the hood of his coat. 'I'd better be going, anyway.'

Carolyn's eyes narrowed. 'What's that?'

Millie looked down at the warm glass in her hand. 'Oh—'

The door banged again and her father was there, misted with rain, his mouth twisted. He looked into the lounge room, the space between him and Carolyn showing they'd fought in the car.

'What's going on?'

'Jem wanted to see the puppies,' Millie repeated. 'We just had a quick look. He heard about them from Zac.'

'Who?' Carolyn asked.

Millie's father steam-rolled over the top of his wife. 'I told you not to manhandle them.'

'He wants to buy one.'

'They can't leave their mother yet.'

'Later,' Millie said, aware that the visitor was shaking his head hard, like a dog. 'When they're ready to go.'

'Who's Zac?' Carolyn asked again.

'I'm not interested,' Jem was saying. He tried to step forward but Millie's parents wouldn't yield the space. 'Got the wrong info.'

'Zac, the butcher,' Millie told her stepmother.

'Well it's good you're not interested, mate,' Millie's father snarled. 'Be even better if you weren't interested in giving my daughter liquor.'

'You're confused, old man,' Jem told the carpet.

Millie's dad bent closer, eyes fiery. 'What's that?'

'It's a misunderstanding,' Jem said more loudly. 'I don't want a dog. I'd better go.'

The back of his throat rumbling like Bella protecting her puppies, Millie's father shifted to one side and allowed the younger man to squeeze between him and Carolyn. Jem slid out the front door like smoke.

Her father shook his head. 'Jesus Christ, Millie.'

'I didn't drink anything,' she protested.

He loped down the hall to the kitchen without responding. Millie heard the fridge door open and the clinking of glass as he retrieved both beers at once. He stomped over the lino to the rumpus room, and a moment later the sound of the TV news pounded through the house.

Outside, the rain picked up again. The visitor, riding home, would be soaked.

Carolyn was still in the entranceway. She stared at Millie as if she were solving a complex mental calculation. At last she said, 'Zac isn't someone you want as a friend.'

'I've never met him.'

'He's a *negative personality.*'

'He told Jem you're nice.'

'I don't need boys like that to think I'm nice.'

A delayed fear whistled through Millie. She took a step towards Carolyn, her mother substitute, and opened her mouth. Carolyn crossed her arms, lips thin with annoyance. 'Did you do anything?'

'*No*,' Millie insisted, the half-empty liquor glass slipping in her sweaty hand, the backs of her thighs cold beneath the too-short skirt. She hunched her shoulders. 'No, I wouldn't.'

Carolyn regarded her for a second longer.

'Change out of your uniform, please,' she instructed, then went to join her husband.

Cheeks burning, Millie took the dirty glass to the kitchen and ran scalding water to shear out every last trace. In the adjoining room the news ended with the blast of brass instruments, then changed to current affairs.

After putting the clean glass back, Millie went to the laundry to check on the puppies. When she clicked on the light the tiny bundles began to twitch and chitter. The stink of milk and blood and puppy shit rose up like a weather front. Millie located the two females and lifted them to her face, rolling her cheeks on their warm backs, then returned them to the others and tucked in the loose blankets to keep them safe.

Bella shuffled over to supervise, her swollen teats swinging, and they both stared down into the box. Tears pricked Millie's eyes as she thought of separating the pups from their mother. Handing them to strangers could give them any kind of life.

She reached down to fit her hand around the familiar curve of her best girl's skull, and Bella nuzzled into her. It had to happen, Millie knew. It was children who thought things could stay the same, and she wasn't a child anymore.

Honey

Casper is sorting through old photographs when the neighbour's dog comes back. She announces herself in the usual way, with deep wet snuffles under the door strung between irritated grunts. He pauses, hoping she might go away, but then her nails start to click against the metal and his heart drops. Yesterday, he swore he'd say something if it happened again, and here's the dog now, a whine starting in her throat. It's the fourth morning in a row.

The events of the weekend must have unsettled her. On Saturday night there'd been noises outside, footsteps and a few banging sounds, but from his bed Casper couldn't tell where they were coming from. The next day a police car parked at the verge and two officers went into Michelle's place. They stayed for thirty-five minutes. Then, on Monday, the dog started scratching at the door.

Casper's street is usually quiet. As those who've been there longest – forty-two years in the same house, since the day after they got married – he and his wife have encouraged this quality. 'The Golden

Rule of neighbourliness,' he's joked to Jan. 'Leave others alone, as you would want to be left alone.' He's happy to smile and nod hello at a fellow resident, learn their first names, memorise their cars, but after that he gives them space and expects it in return. If he wanted people in his business all the time, he'd move to a retirement village.

Still, he's seen *A Current Affair*, winced at the screaming matches over the tops of fences. Property can produce disputes out of thin air. The arrangement they have is especially risky, with Casper's house at the front of the block and Michelle renting the unit behind. When the police arrived on Saturday, they walked up the shared driveway, passing Casper's lounge room window. The officers' individual foot-falls were soft and regular on the bitumen, the *ke-ke ke-ke* of a steady moving train.

The dog, Honey, is a lovely animal, a yellow Lab with emotive brown eyes. She sits obediently when Casper opens the back door, revealing her on the other side of the flywire.

'Hello, girl,' he whispers, knowing Jan wouldn't approve. Jan is no animal lover. The only pets the family ever had were two goldfish, Bubble and Squeak, and those were meant to be cared for by their daughters – although they never did, as kids don't.

The fish died of starvation in a dirty tank, with each girl blaming the other for the neglect. Jan had been appalled. 'You each walked past them twenty times a day, and you never even looked in to see how they were doing?' There were no more pets after that.

Now she knows Casper's there, Honey will be patient while he finds her something to eat. Unused to dogs, it took Casper a while to figure out what she wanted the first time she turned up: he told her to go home, patted her, told her to go home, threw a tennis ball, gave her a dish of water, told her to go home, and even tried to lead her by the collar back to Michelle's before he realised she might be hungry. She ran off after he offered two old carrots from the fridge, the sticks wedged under her lip like tusks. The determination with which she gulps down his scraps is a bit of a worry. Yesterday, Wednesday, she nearly choked with enthusiasm over two stale end-slices of bread.

From the kitchen he brings back a browning apple core and his unfinished bowl of Weet-Bix. Honey's nose is in the cereal as soon as he opens the wire door. He strokes the back of her neck while she eats, listening to her chops slopping up the half-dried mush. 'What's wrong, Hon?' he murmurs.

Michelle screamed at the dog on Tuesday. He's never heard her do that before; really, for the three years she and Honey have lived there, they've been exemplary. Michelle doesn't even have a car. All they hear is heels on the drive when she comes and goes from work and her soft chatter to the dog as they leave for evening walks.

When Jan first found out that the new tenant was bringing a dog she predicted barking and upheaval. 'A Labrador?' she complained to Casper when Michelle and Honey arrived, the dog happily trailing their movers between the van and the front door. 'There isn't enough room.'

Casper disagreed, reminding her of the property's slate floors and long, thin backyard. 'A good dog will go okay.'

Jan snorted. 'No such thing,' she'd said, and pulled the blind shut.

When the dog got yelled at, Casper was out the back, taking advantage of the cool evening to get some weeding done. Michelle's voice was strained like she was close to tears: '*For fuck's sake, you stupid dog, get out, get OUT!*'

Casper kept his eyes on his plants. None of his business, he told himself.

'*Stupid fucking dog, STUPID FUCKING DOG, OUT!*'

It only lasted a few minutes. When he was sure it was over, Casper tried to look on the bright side. Until then, he hadn't heard anything from Michelle since the weekend. At least she was still alive.

Honey crunches through the last half of apple core and looks up expectantly. Her tail twitches when Casper zips his jacket and extends to full wag when he steps outside. She follows him across the lawn but stops when they get to the driveway.

'Come on, let's see if your mum's home,' he says cheerily, but Honey lowers her bum, doubtful. 'Come on, girl.'

The dog doesn't move.

With a sigh, he goes to Michelle's gate and sees that it's unlatched. Honey must be able to get her nose between the bars and pull it open. 'Clever dog,' he murmurs, watching her come up the drive towards him. 'Good girl.' They go through the gate.

It was he and Jan who'd had the unit built. They'd subdivided twelve years ago when their daughters had left home and Jan was feeling depressed. Up and down the street families were knocking over the original dwellings and putting up narrow townhouses on the quarter-acre blocks, but Casper couldn't bear to share a wall. He'd despised living on a building site, workmen going in and out, pushing dirt under the back door. Jan, on the other hand, had thrown herself into the planning, choosing the design and all the fixtures and fittings, down to blinds and door handles. Really, what she wanted was for them to swap, to live in the fresh new unit and sell the more valuable home at the front, but Casper put his foot down. He couldn't live tucked in behind another family, watching them redo his life.

He also didn't want to be landlord to someone living ten metres from his back door, so they sold the unit to a thirty-five year old investor who wore a polo shirt and shorts. When they met, and it was only the one time, Casper had asked him to please be mindful of them when choosing his tenants. Jan was embarrassed but the investor gave them a broad smile. 'You're one of my selling points,' he said, clapping an arm around Casper's shoulders. 'Nice retired couple living in front, no pets, no kids? You're part of the package, mate!'

'We should introduce him to the girls,' Jan joked to Casper after the papers were signed. 'A man with money.'

'I don't want a son-in-law who gets rich off of my property,' Casper had grumbled. 'Not before I'm even dead.'

Despite his smarmy appearance, the investor had kept his word: the first tenants were a childless couple whose sole crime was playing jazz CDs in the evenings, followed by a friendly single bloke who worked three weeks of the month on an oil rig and spent his week off sleeping and playing video games. When he shifted to Queensland, Michelle moved in.

Hesitating at the door, Casper palpates the scruff of Honey's neck. She gives a soft creaking groan and pushes back against his hand. The outside of the property bears no sign of what might have happened on Saturday. 'Better get your mum, then,' he says to Honey, and knocks.

There is shuffling inside the unit. Eventually, the main door opens but Michelle stays behind the security grille. She is wearing the top and bottom of two different tracksuits.

He knows very little about Michelle, of course. She lives alone, with a dog, and works a nine-to-five job somewhere on the bus route; she looks to be in her mid-thirties, like his daughters. In the past he brought up her spinsterhood with Jan, more out of curiosity than anything, but his wife had been hostile, for once, to the gossip. 'Not everyone needs to get married, you know,' she said. 'Women can do what they like these days.'

He seems to remember Jan taking a different attitude to their girls. 'It's just nice to have a partner,' he'd defended. 'Don't you think?'

'If you can find a good one.' The degree of Jan's irritation was unusual. He touched her hand. 'Just leave the girl alone,' she continued, shaking him off. 'She's living her life. She's free.'

The Michelle he's looking at now doesn't seem very free. 'Hi, Casper,' she greets, warily. She notices the dog hovering at his side. 'Honey,' she says, and the pup presses into Casper with concern.

She opens the security door for Honey, who won't go in. With the wire mesh gone, Casper can see Michelle more clearly. Her hair is unbrushed, her face pale. 'You alright, love?' he asks.

Michelle pats her hair self-consciously. 'I'm fine.' She looks at Honey. 'Get inside,' she commands, and when the Lab is too slow, 'Move!'

Casper watches Honey tiptoe into the unit and wonders if it has all the original décor – the carpet, the tiles, the wall paint Jan chose, poring over brochures with joy in her eyes. She should have designed the insides of houses professionally, but that wasn't a job when they were young. Lord knows their house has always been impeccable, with Jan sewing new covers for the lounge suite and upgrading their bedding in the January sales. She'd kept house, had two kids and spent thirty-four years as the secretary for a podiatrist; Casper wonders what Michelle would think of a life like that.

'Did you need something?' the neighbour asks now. She holds the security door half-open, so as not to be rude. She seems on edge.

'Sorry, love, but the dog's been at the back door the last few days. I think you've forgotten to lock the gate.'

Michelle seems unsurprised. 'Oh,' she says. 'Sorry about that.'

Casper isn't sure how to proceed. He doesn't want to mention what he heard on the weekend, the police visit, before she does. 'It's not really a bother,' he says at last. 'Poor pup just seemed hungry. I gave her some food. I hope that's alright.'

'I'm sorry,' the neighbour says again, but her voice isn't as dispassionate this time. She drops her gaze and it takes a second for Casper to realise she's crying.

He feels terrible now, a solid trunk of awful from shoulders to knees, and can't think what to do. In the past he's responded to his daughters' and granddaughters' tears appropriately, hugging them, rubbing the wet tracks back into their flushed skin, but this is the longest conversation he's ever had with Michelle. It doesn't seem right to touch her.

'Never mind,' he says, after a moment. Down the hallway he can see the dog's eyes glinting. 'It's fine, really.'

She stops crying and asks if he'd like to come in. He would not, but he can't very well refuse. Michelle locks both doors behind them.

Inside, the kitchen is the same one Jan had put in: a dove-coloured countertop over blond timber cupboards. Country style, she called it. In the dining space are a small glass table and two chairs. Casper sits down. Michelle brings him some tap water and then stands behind the breakfast bar. He drinks to fill time. Jan must be wondering what on earth is going on.

'I'm sorry about Honey,' Michelle says. Her third apology.

The dog is lying under the table, her warm throat against Casper's ankle. He feels the vibration of her breath, like a cat's purr. 'It's really okay,' he says. 'I was just worried that if she could get out, she might run off while you were at work.'

His neighbour doesn't say she hasn't been at work. It's eleven o'clock in the morning.

He finishes his water and she comes around to get his glass, saying, 'I can pay for the food you gave her.'

'Oh, heavens, no, no. It would've gone into compost otherwise.'

'Would you like a sandwich?'

The change in focus is sudden and Casper doesn't follow until she lifts a loaf of bread from the bench. 'Oh, no, I'm fine, thank you.'

Michelle shrugs and puts it back down. It was her idea for him to come inside and, presumably, talk, but she isn't giving him much to go on. Eventually, he asks, 'Is everything okay, love?'

She doesn't answer. Instead, she says, 'Has anyone been giving you trouble?'

The second abrupt shift confuses him again. 'What do you mean?'

'No-one's come to the house, nicked anything, stuff like that?'

He's so flabbergasted he can only shrug. Is that what happened on the weekend? For some reason he thought the problem, whatever it'd been, was internal. Personal. There's never been a burglary on the street before, and the police didn't say anything, never warned him to be on the lookout. He tries to remember if he locked the front door today.

Michelle sighs and goes over to the sink. She turns on the hot tap and squeezes a bottle of dishwashing liquid into it. 'No-one's come over?' she asks again. 'No-one's been hassling you?'

He chuckles grimly. 'No-one's come to my house for a while, love.'

Almost to herself, she says, 'He said he'd get at you.'

'What's that?'

Michelle picks up a handful of dirty forks and spoons. 'I wonder if maybe Honey could stay with you,' she says, her voice raised, and dumps the cutlery in the sink.

Jan wouldn't approve, Casper thinks. He looks down at the dog. She looks back with damp eyes. 'Are you going somewhere?'

Michelle shrugs, pushing up the sleeves of her windcheater. Grey bruises bracelet her wrists.

Honey quivers against Casper's leg and he realises the dog is afraid. He reaches to pat her, wondering what is going on in this unit.

'Things aren't good right now,' Michelle says. 'I don't think Honey should stay here.' She hauls cups and plates out of the water and pushes them along the draining board. 'I left the gate open so she'd run away.'

Honey grumbles deep in her abdomen when he pulls his hand back. 'Why did the police come?'

Michelle shakes her head and keeps washing dishes. Steam rises from them thickly; her hands must sting.

Casper would like to go back to his own house. This is why he's tried to keep a friendly distance from his neighbours. People seem nice, but if you get involved in their lives this is what you find.

'I thought you might be lonely,' Michelle says after a while. She's facing the window and he has to ask her to repeat herself. 'Honey could keep you company.'

He pushes his chair back from the table. 'I think I'd better be going.'

Michelle puts down her tea towel and turns to him. 'We're neighbours, aren't we?' She runs a swollen pink finger over the mark on one wrist. 'We should be able to ask each other for help.'

'Do you need help?' he asks stiffly.

'What about you?'

Honey butts Casper's calf with her nose and looks at him mournfully. He rubs between her shoulders. 'I'm not sure what you mean.'

'I never asked how you were when your wife died.'

Casper's hand freezes in Honey's fur.

'I know we don't talk much, but Jan was very kind to me.'

He clears his throat. 'She was a kind person.'

'She used to give me advice.'

Just leave the girl alone, he remembers his wife telling him. Two years ago: she was well then. *She's living her life. She's free.* Now Jan is free as well.

'I tell myself she's still here,' he finds himself telling the neighbour, looking through the glass tabletop at the tiles Jan had chosen. 'It's too hard otherwise.'

Michelle comes over and sits at the table across from him. 'Would you rather just be left alone?'

'Well, love,' he says, stroking the soft folds around Honey's neck. 'Maybe we can look after one another.'

Baby

To work off her late-afternoon agitation, Marla calls for her daughter's dog, who's out in the long grass snapping at moths. Baby bounds in, her great mouth leaking, shivering with excitement as Marla tries to snap on her lead. When she bends forward to grip the dog's collar the stitches along Marla's panty line twang in protest. 'Babe. Come on, girl. I'm doing this for you.'

Fi's dog has the dense brow of a Neanderthal and a loose rooster's wattle, but she's a gentle animal. When the lead is finally secured, she leans forward, tongue lolling, and breathes appreciation into Marla's face. Grimacing, Marla steadies Baby's snout, looping around it the halter that prevents her from pulling when she sees another dog. Although the straps are only designed to press discouragingly against her skin, passers-by sometimes mistake them for Hannibal Lecter's muzzle. 'She's not dangerous!' Marla has called to women turning back their strollers when they see big Baby grunting with excitement. At the park, other owners lead their dogs in the opposite direction, distrustful of the straps around Baby's jaw. Baby would love to play but there's no point explaining, so Marla makes a point of leading her away.

If Fi had asked her advice Marla would never have encouraged adopting such a large animal. The food bills alone are enormous, along with the piles of excrement that result. Now Fi is gone, and Baby's kibble and turds are Marla's responsibility. She's done her best to live up to it, taking the dog out at least once a day, ever since the doctors gave her the all-clear. She wonders if her daughter was as diligent.

Today they take a new route, Baby and Marla, grandmother and grand-dog, as Fi has sometimes referred to them. Marla knows her daughter won't be having her own children but she finds it cruel for her to imply that Baby is a reasonable substitute. Marla is good with little children; she likes them. She would have been a good grandmother. Maybe a better grandmother than a mother.

It's quiet as she and Baby weave through the suburb, walking down the middle of roads because they can, the bright cars motionless in their drive-ways. It's six-thirty, dinnertime for families, and humid enough to scare away cyclists and joggers. In the distance, Marla hears whistles and faint cheers from a sports field or open swimming pool. There's a thrum of vehicles from a nearby main road, but on the cul-de-sacs and loops there is only the sound of Baby's dinner-plate paws padding on the bitumen and the hot rushes of her breath around the harness.

Fifteen minutes into their stroll the sutures pull in Marla's abdomen and she stops to gently stretch, one hand in the small of her back. Although she's inspected the site many times over the past two weeks, running a finger over the whorls as if tracing a sentence, Marla keeps getting the sensation that the filaments are tightening. From the outside things seem to be healing as predicted, the surrounding skin its normal hue except for slivers of redness right where the open curtains of her flesh have been pulled back together. For the first few days the wound itched and she stood erect in front of the TV, running her fingers over the bandage and meditating on the idea that she mustn't scratch. Baby lay in her beanbag on the carpet, entranced by Marla's slow stroking.

When the bandage was removed, the itch went away. Marla thought the worst was over, but still the stitches snag on nothing, tug randomly, burn in jagged flashes of lightning. She tightens her lips against the sudden pain and assumes this is part of the healing process. Tomorrow she will go back and have the sutures snipped out so that only the pinkish raised flesh is left, like a snarl. She is hoping for a scar.

The dog is patient as Marla checks the wound, the leash slack between them. Saliva drips from the baggy corners of her mouth like tears. 'Good girl,' Marla says, reaching for the dense skull. 'You're a good girl.' She massages Baby's occiput the way she likes it.

Fiona's dog tilts back on her hindquarters and lifts her front legs as if to wrap Marla in a hug. 'Hey, hey,' Marla warns, stepping back from the dirt and piss and gravel now lodged in the crevices of Baby's mighty paws. The dog loses her balance, her heavy front half sweeping back down with gravity. The thick dark nails of Baby's front-left paw drag down Marla's sutures and sever them.

Marla presses both hands to her belly as if her guts are going to tumble out. 'Fuck!' she screams. 'Baby!'

Admonished, the dog skitters back, pulling the lead from Marla's loose grip. A pulse of pain runs through her wound and the hem of her top feels wet, but when she checks it's only sweat and a stripe of mud from Baby's paw. She lifts her head again and sees the dog already halfway down the road, galloping out of sight.

'Baby!' she yells. 'Baby, back!'

She knows she should give chase, but first she lifts her shirt away and squints in the lessening light, trying to examine the injury. Two weeks ago she did the same thing, curling forward to see how deep it was, the blood sluicing down her abdomen.

The wound is much the same as it was a minute ago. There's no blood. A single suture has been sliced through by Baby's fingernail, the two ends sticking up like wires.

Relieved, Marla straightens. On the opposite side of the road a young girl, eight or nine years old, is straddling a scooter in her family's carport. 'What are you doing?' the kid demands.

Marla tries to smile. 'Sorry, I was just looking at something.'

'In your *pants*,' the girl says contemptuously. She grips the handlebars and rocks the scooter hard.

Marla walks towards her. 'Did you see my dog?'

'Dog?' The girl sounds dubious.

Marla realises that this is the kind of thing kidnappers say to children: *I have a puppy in my van; do you want to see?* She taught Fiona about stranger danger many times. 'If anyone makes you feel uncomfortable, you can tell them to leave you alone,' she insisted, holding her daughter's hand tight.

Fi, the same age as this girl, rolled her eyes. Her ponytail was clean and blond, her eyes blue. The hair along her arms shone gold in the daylight. In her school pictures she looked like a child who was already missing. 'I'm uncomfortable, Mum,' she said drolly. 'Leave me alone.'

'Never mind,' Marla tells the neighbour. 'It's okay. I'll find her.'

The girl shrugs, disinterested. She plants a foot on the base of her scooter and rolls into the driveway.

Marla goes up the street and around the corner Baby took, sure she'll find the animal cowering by a streetlight or squatting to release hot urine on the road. Baby has bolted a couple of times before, but if there's nothing to chase she doesn't get far: after a few hundred metres she slows and looks back, then stops. A young man at work once showed Marla pictures on the internet of dogs stuck in sofas or on top of high surfaces, each featuring the caption *I forgot how to dog*. It's what Marla thinks of when she sees Baby lose interest in her freedom and wait to be recaptured.

She's had to work this out about Baby, along with the rest of it. When she picked the dog up from Fi's she'd already been alone for a couple of days. After the half-hour ordeal of getting Baby into her hatchback, Marla went back into the empty house, searching cupboards until she found the big bag of kibble and scouring under the sofa and beds for Baby's toys. On the highway she realised she'd left the food bowls behind but couldn't bear to go back. The pet shop had a set on sale – creamy ceramic with *Feed me* and *Water me* stencilled in baby blue on the sides.

The *I forgot how to dog* colleague suggested pigs' ears, so Marla buys bags of them for when she needs ten minutes to herself. She suspects she gives Baby too many, like a parent doling out chocolate bars to a whingeing kid, but she feels bad for the dog. Baby faces rejection wherever she goes: her first couple of owners; the weeks at the animal refuge; the humans and animals who panic when she approaches. And now Fiona. 'Mummy didn't abandon you,' Marla wants to tell her. 'She didn't want to go.' Instead, she communicates by handing over the shell of dried ear-skin, so fresh and disgusting there are bristles still clumped in a corner.

The street ends and Marla turns right. Passing two cul-de-sacs, she stops at the entrance to each and calls for Baby but hears nothing. At a Give Way sign she turns left, a sense of hopelessness growing in her. Marla doesn't recognise the area. She hasn't come to any major roads; she hasn't passed any shops or parks. The rumble of far-off traffic is making her crazy. At the next side street, she stands in the middle of the bitumen and cups her hands to her mouth. 'Bay-bee!' she screams. 'Come – the fuck – *out!*'

'Are you right?'

It takes her a while to find the source of the voice. Two houses up, a young woman hangs over the railing of a narrow balcony. The sunlight glints off something she is holding. Squinting, Marla calls, 'Hello?'

The woman shifts the object to her other hand but doesn't respond. Marla walks towards her house like a lost child approaching an adult at the shops, stopping at the kerb. The young woman gazes down at her like Juliet. 'What?'

'Sorry, I thought you asked if I was alright.' Marla laughs, uncertain.

'I said, are you *right.*' She steps back and arranges her hair over her shoulders. She is as peevish as the little girl on the scooter. 'As in, do you mind?'

'*Are you right,*' Marla repeats. She looks back up the street. '*Do you mind.* It's all in the way you say it, isn't it?'

The younger woman arches her back and shakes her head. Marla realises the shiny thing is a wineglass when the woman waves it at her. 'What's your problem?'

'I've lost my daughter's dog,' Marla responds. Saying it makes her want to cry. She walks onto the front lawn. 'Did you see a dog come past here?'

The front door to the house opens and another, older, woman takes a step across the threshold. Her beckoning leg bends daintily like a ballet dancer's, going *en pointe* in white rubber thongs. Her hair is curly like the woman's upstairs. 'Can I help you?' she asks Marla.

'She lost a dog,' the young woman shouts down, as if her mother is deaf.

The older woman's feathery eyebrows lift, but not out of concern for Baby. Still gazing at Marla, she calls, 'What's that, Ellie?'

'Lost her *dog.*'

'Lost your dog?' The woman twists her proffered knee and Marla sees a pink line through the centre of it. She's had an operation. Marla wonders if the daughter, Ellie, looks after her.

'She isn't dangerous,' Marla explains. 'Usually she's very well behaved.'

'Usually?' the woman asks.

'Basically always.'

'What does she *look* like, though?' Ellie calls down.

'Well, a bit like a Rottweiler, but with Staffy colouring. She's blue.'

'What, like a Smurf?'

Marla speaks to the mother. 'It's a grey colour, but they call it blue.'

The older woman shakes her head.

A few droplets hit Marla from above, and she glances up. It's Ellie, tipping her glass. 'Oops,' the younger woman says vaguely. 'Sorry.'

Even though it's just a couple of drops of wine, Marla is repulsed by the sensation, as if Ellie has spit on her. She shakes her head forcefully. 'Well, you obviously haven't seen her, so—'

'What's her name?' Ellie interrupts.

'Her name? Baby.'

Ellie snorts. The mother tilts her head in her daughter's direction, like the dog does when Marla talks to her. 'Oh,' the mother says. 'Funny.'

'We got her from a refuge,' Marla explains. She notices she's used the plural pronoun and the skin around her stitches tingles. 'They'd already named her.'

'Where'd you lose her?' Ellie asks.

'A few blocks away.'

Ellie lowers herself so that her youthful bosoms rest on the balcony's railing. She is younger than Fiona; Marla guesses twenty-five, twenty-six. But the mother seems old.

'How d'you know she came this way?'

'I saw her.'

'Not for long,' Ellie points out.

Something whines past Marla's ear and stings the back of her neck. She slaps it away and feels the stickiness of her sweat. She realises how dark it's getting. 'I should really go.'

As if she hasn't spoken, Ellie asks, 'How old's Baby?'

'What?'

'Is she a puppy?'

'No. She's a mature dog.'

'And she ran away?'

'She was scared.'

'Of what?'

Marla looks to Ellie's mother for help. The woman blinks and straightens her leg, then extends the other one slowly and brushes her toes against the doormat.

By now Marla thinks that Baby must be gone, bundled into a ranger's van for snapping at a poodle or hit by a tradie's ute on the highway. 'She was just scared,' she murmurs.

'Well,' the older woman says abruptly, pulling her leg inside, 'I've got to make the tea. I hope you find your dog,' she says to Marla, her expression flat. She shuts the door.

'So the dog's not dangerous?' Ellie calls down.

Marla sighs but answers, as if being questioned by police. 'She looks scary but she's never bitten anyone.'

'A lot of people say that.' Ellie straightens her back, both palms pressing down on the railing. 'They pretend their dogs aren't vicious.'

'Well, mine isn't.'

Ellie gazes down at her like a queen from a throne.

'Are you scared of dogs?' Marla asks.

In the younger woman's silence Marla feels a rush of energy, as if she's finally pinned her. She smiles. She remembers arguing with Fi when she was younger, the teenager trying to twist her arguments in on themselves, to prove her mother was a hypocrite just like everyone else.

Ellie smiles down at her cruelly. 'Not when they're muzzled.'

'It's not a muzzle, it's—' Marla stops, the power draining from her. 'You saw the dog.'

Ellie withdraws from the balcony, the glass door sliding shut behind her. Marla waits. More mosquitoes pierce her cheeks, her upper arms, her shins. She presses a fingertip to the spot on her belly where Baby's nail sliced the stitch in two and feels a tiny tack of drying blood.

There is the click of a gate, then footsteps through the darkness. Marla hears rough panting.

'Baby?'

The dog whines, straining for Marla, but Ellie holds her back by the collar.

'Is this your dog?'

'Don't be fucking stupid.'

Baby is released and she rushes for Marla, who sinks to her knees and lets the hot belly press into her, flat tongue searching Marla's ears, paws scrabbling at her breasts and shoulders. Marla holds the wiggling animal close, not caring when her sharp canine knees push into her wound and desperate back claws drag against the inside of her thighs. Finally, Baby settles and Marla stands up again, half of her head lacquered by dog spit, not nearly as bloodcurdling as Ellie's discarded wine.

'I was so worried.' In the dark she can't see the younger woman but feels her presence, strong and repellent.

'Should keep a better eye on your dog,' Ellie says.

'You said it yourself. You wouldn't be so brave if she wasn't in a harness.' Marla wraps the end of the leash tight around her palm like a boxer strapping up. 'You'd piss your pants like a little girl.'

Baby leads them home, keeping close to the kerb and waiting at intersections as if she knows Marla can't take much more. Halfway back Marla stops the dog to remove the restraint from her face, and though she shakes her jowls for a moment, Baby doesn't pull once.

At home Marla pours Baby's kibble onto the kitchen floor and watches, smiling, as the dog rolls around in it, flicking her tongue at the dark brown balls. When she's finished, Marla uses scissors to remove the plastic from a pig's ear and sinks down against the cabinets to watch Baby eat it. Fi's dog lies spreadeagled on the tiles, a protective paw held to her snout, and Marla laughs.

'I won't steal it, Babe.' Tears itch her eyes. 'No-one's going to take it away from you.' She looks at the ceiling to stop from crying and thinks of Fi, something she hasn't allowed herself to do since it happened.

Even when her daughter was waving the knife, Marla hadn't really believed she would do anything. Instead of stepping back she kept approaching, thinking her calmness would be convincing. 'Fi,' she'd said. Fiona had been erratic before, but this was different. 'Fi, come on.' Startled, Fi slashed the air like an explorer clearing the jungle, and the tip of the blade sliced through the fabric of Marla's dress and into the skin below. Marla knew she hadn't meant to do it, but when Fi bolted from the house she asked triple-zero for the police before the ambulance because her daughter still had the knife. When the officers cornered Fi in the backyard she waved it in their direction, and that was a second crime.

After the wound – surprisingly shallow, but long – had been stitched up, Marla phoned the switchboard of the facility where the police took Fi, but she was advised to give it more time. A day later she remembered the dog, still locked in Fi's laundry. When Marla entered the house she saw the smashed wineglass on the coffee table and dots of blood in the carpet.

The pig's ear finished, Baby crosses the room and drops her massive head into Marla's lap. Marla bends forward to embrace her and winces as her stitches pull tight.

'Up, Babe,' she instructs, and the dog stands reluctantly. 'Good girl. Just a second.'

Marla retrieves the scissors and folds back her dirty T-shirt. Carefully, she snips through the remaining sutures, feeling the relief of the threads sliding out. The scar is pearlescent in the light. When she's finished, she tucks the scissors behind her and opens her arms to the dog. 'Come on, Baby,' she says. 'Come to Grandma.'

The Spaniel

During winter, when heavy rains turned the school oval to mud and everyone was kept inside on a lightning warning, Nathan Shenton's Year Seven sports class watched puberty movies in the gym. Thank God this class was boys only – he seriously would've died if he'd had to sit next to a girl, tensing his thigh so their knees didn't touch, and watch the same screen as a pimply kid lifted his shirt to reveal a dense grove of black hair in his armpits. *For boys*, the voiceover said, *hair is likely to coarsen and darken all over your body, but especially on your face, chest, under your arms, and around your genitals.*

Nope. No! Nathan imagined his own armpits, fuzzy blond at best, almost smooth, layered with strong-smelling deodorant every morning. He touched his soft cheek and kept his thoughts above his waist.

School was co-ed and Anglican; you had to wear a blazer and black shoes, but individual hairstyles and accessories were allowed. At the moment, other boys were growing their hair and brushing it down over one eye to get the uninterested look. Girls flat-ironed long ponytails, flipped them over one shoulder and stroked them like fur collars. Everyone performed their boredom. Nathan's hair was still short and gelled upwards like dozens of raised eyebrows, which was last year's look.

The following week, rolls of thunder could be heard over the hum of the gym lights as their teacher, Mr Miller, struggled to get an old DVD to play without skipping. Finally, the image of a party-popper surfaced on the screen, coloured in lurid pink and purple. It jittered for a moment and then burst, ejecting thin white streamers. A synthesised beat started up as the streamers spread and danced around, at last spelling out the title of the movie: Tony's Story.

Nathan put his elbows on his knees and leaned forward. He loved it when class time was given over to watching movies, though not for the usual reasons. He was going to be an actor one day and knew he'd have to start out small, maybe in one of these educational videos. His favourite was the one on saying no to peer pressure that they'd watched in Health. He could be one of the guys who pushed away an iPhone with a naked shot of a girl from school. 'Dude, that isn't cool,' he'd say. 'Respect her right to privacy, man.'

They sat on the cool floor of the gym and huddled into their jackets. The side entrance kept opening as staff used the thoroughfare to avoid the weather. A youngish, good-looking Maths teacher crossed the back of the room, and some of the boys noticed and called out. She waved before leaving, a cold draught washing in behind her. Despite the moving air and high ceilings, the place still carried the sharp hormonal stink of caged teens.

On the TV a young man appeared, his hair dark and curly like the armpits the previous week. Hi, he said. *You want to hear a funny story? A story* – the actor paused and the music stopped – *about erections?*

The gymnasium exploded with yells and whoops. At the back, a row of popular boys drummed their sneakered feet against the wooden floor. Nathan's pure armpits dripped.

'Quiet,' Mr Miller growled in his thick Scottish accent, turning the sound up on the TV. 'Yeh'll want to watch this so as not to embarrass ye'selves.'

Nathan sat up straighter. He was very interested in tips on how not to embarrass himself. As the other kids elbowed one another over an anatomical drawing onscreen, Nathan felt embarrassed to have to sit in a clot of goony boys to learn how to avoid embarrassment.

Tony's Story was about Tony, the curly-haired smiley guy, who was relatively popular until he got an erection in class one day. It cut between scenes of Tony sitting at a desk, reddening, unable to stand up when the bell rang, and him talking to the camera, a half-smile on his face: *I thought I was the only person it'd ever happened to.* Tony shook his head to indicate that this wasn't true. Nathan snuck a look to see if anyone else appeared to agree, but his classmates just seemed grossed out and delighted.

As the characters got up for their next class, a guy Tony thought was his friend spotted him and began to laugh. *Hey, everyone, Tony's got an erection!* he announced. Other students gathered and pointed. Gathered and pointed! The camera panned around the room – the teacher had mysteriously gone. *Erection! Erec-tion!* the rest of Tony's class were chanting, which even Nathan thought was unlikely. Still, the sense of contagion made him anxious. His own class was giggling.

The camera began to spin in a circle from Tony's point of view, the faces of his former friends flashing past. Nathan got dizzy. Finally, the movement stopped and Tony's face filled the screen, staring right at him. *It was the worst day of my life*, he told Nathan gravely.

Tony was unpopular and unhappy for a whole day. Then, when the bell rang the next morning, he noticed his former mate, his tormentor, not moving from his seat. As everyone else got up, the mate looked at Tony imploringly.

Nathan's classmates began to holler 'Erection! Erection!' like lunatics. Mr Miller rolled his eyes and sipped his Nescafé. On the television Tony paused for a moment, then nodded at his friend. *Come on, guys, let's go*, he instructed those milling about the classroom, and even though he'd been the butt of their jokes for twenty-four hours, they listened. When the others had filed out into the hall Tony stopped in the doorway and turned to the friend, who was still at his desk, shame on his face. Their eyes met. Then Tony followed the rest of the students out of the room.

'Wait,' one of the boy's in Nathan's class shouted. 'So they just left him behind to jerk off?'

The others went nuts. Mr Miller stood up in exasperation, slopping coffee out of his mug, and switched the DVD off. 'Right, yer little gasbags,' he ordered, pointing to the other end of the gym. 'If ye' can't behave ye'selves, do sprints.'

The boys got off the floor and jogged half-heartedly from one basketball ring to another, still sniggering. On the far edge of the group, Nathan put his head down and ran fast, trying to push the image of those spinning, screaming faces out of his mind.

After that, it stopped raining and real Phys. Ed. resumed. No-one else seemed affected by Tony's story: in the change rooms they pulled off their clothes as they'd always done, pausing in their jocks to unselfconsciously scratch the hair on their stomachs and under their arms.

But Nathan saw threats everywhere. His body was still lithe and white but other curses were descending. He went to answer a teacher's question and the pitch of his voice fumbled, shivering into its correct notch. He rubbed his sore chin and the next day there was a throbbing whitehead that disappeared only to resurface on his cheek, the tip of his nose, between his eyes. He stood in the shower at home, wasting water, trying to decide if his nipples were changing colour.

The biggest danger, though, was what had happened to Tony. Nathan didn't have brothers and hung around mostly with girls, so he had an indefinite understanding of what the thing between his legs was capable of. His dad, who usually liked to over-explain things in the hope this would make them okay, had so far managed to avoid the topic, and Nathan wanted it to stay that way. He did not want to talk about it with anyone.

At school you could only be known for a couple of traits – teenagers already had enough to worry about without being forced to recognise that personalities were multifaceted and ultimately unknowable, so they held one another down with crude pins. Nathan's were that he was small and liked theatre. This pushed him towards unpopularity, but as long as other kids could be diagnosed fat, stupid or gay he wasn't a main target. He was abused casually if he came into a bully's line of sight, and he'd learned that acceptable reactions fit into a slim window: push back too much and the bullies enjoyed it; too little and it pissed them off. So far, he'd kept within the limits, but what if the soft curled snail in his pants woke up at school and began to dance? Whoever had written the script for that movie had the right idea about Tony's experience, if not the heroic way he rescued his friend. If there was anything for the other guys to spot, they would, and they'd eat Nathan like sharks.

He remembered the frenzy at the end of the video: 'So they just left him behind to jerk off?' That was another trap. The boys at school were arranged into two groups: the ones who were allowed to, and the ones who weren't. At Monday morning assembly some bragged about weekends spent with their hands in their jocks, filling tissues, beating records. They laughed and knocked shoulders as they talked, trying to push one another off balance.

Others were accused of masturbation like a crime. At recess one day Nathan went to the toilet and found a gang of boys dotted like pimples around the disabled cubicle, banging on the door. 'Whatcha doin' in there, Matty?' they shouted, jumping at the top of the partition, trying to haul themselves up for a look. 'Playing with yourself?'

Bodily functions: what a minefield, now that he was a teenager. Nathan's dad didn't used to care if he let the odd burp slip, when it was just the two of them. Now Rob Shenton furrowed his brow with dismay. 'It's not pleasant, mate,' he muttered, even when Nathan excused himself.

Then, one night, he was in bed with a book and his mother burst in. 'For God's sake,' she seethed. Her eyes were red. 'If I have to clean drops of piss off the toilet floor one more time—'

She held up an old sponge and for a horrifying second Nathan thought she might fling it at him. He sat up, heart hammering. 'Sorry.'

'Sorry, sorry, everyone's always *sorry*,' Laura snapped, and stomped out.

Nathan eased back under the covers and tried to read again, to pretend he was fine. His hands shook. After that, every time he finished, he unwound paper from the roll and wiped down the tiles, even if he didn't see anything, just in case.

But still his mother got angry with him. She didn't like how much gel he put in his hair, the sloppy way he tucked in his shirt, how he left his cereal bowl on the table instead of putting it in the sink, how he left it in the sink instead of putting it in the dishwasher. 'Sorry, Mum,' he said, trying to clean up after himself, tidy things away. 'Sorry.'

'Don't be sorry,' she said. '*Do* something.'

'Sorry.'

She needed someone to fight with after Nathan's older sister had got pregnant, dropped out of TAFE, and moved in with a boyfriend their parents had barely met. Laura oscillated between being furious about Zoey and crying over her. 'She's only nineteen!' she shouted at Rob and Nathan, as if they didn't know. Laura was twenty when she'd had Zoey, but the fact that this turned out okay didn't seem to reassure her. 'What was the point of it?' he'd heard his mother ask his father, the two of them sitting on Zoey's bed, her room across the hall from Nathan's. 'What was even the point?'

Nathan had thought that having a baby in the family might be a cool thing, but he didn't anymore.

In September Nathan was still thinking about *Tony's Story*, still worrying what might happen in an unguarded moment, but things were improving. His pimple had migrated into his left nostril, which hurt like hell but couldn't be seen by other people. He was getting good marks, he had two friends, and his dad had just bought him a mock director's chair from the Reject Shop.

In fact, he didn't think it was over the top to say that today was probably going to be the best day of his life. This morning he'd audition for the Year Seven play, the first real production Nathan and his best friends, Candice and Bree, had ever been in, with costumes and a program and everything. At the same time, Nathan's mother was turning forty and there was a chance that Zoey, whom he hadn't seen for months, would come to the party. Even if she didn't, Bree would definitely be there, since their parents were best mates. He'd been looking forward to it for weeks: the adults would take their wine out to the patio, leaving Nathan and Bree with the house to themselves, bottles of Coke and party pies, and a late-night movie for mature audiences. Lying back on the couch as the lead characters moved their faces together, the music and their hearts both beating faster.

To celebrate, Nathan styled his hair with his favourite wax, which really belonged to Zoey but had a unisex coconut smell. He was trying to use it sparingly. He put on his lucky socks and borrowed Rob's razor to scrape a few blonde hairs off his upper lip. After some consideration he left the sparse strands that grew along his jawline. There was something cool about them.

Outside, Nathan's and Bree's mothers stood on the front lawn beside the Grants' four-wheel drive. Laura held herself around the waist with one arm and blocked the sun from her eyes with the other. Through the car's passenger window Nathan could see Bree.

Bree's mum stopped whatever she'd been saying when she saw Nathan. 'There he is.'

'Hi, Mrs Grant.'

Nathan's parents and Bree's had been friends for ages, since university, and the families' roots grew around one another. They were each other's godparents, emergency contacts, travel buddies. The first photograph of anyone holding Zoey was Caroline Grant, twenty-one with a bad haircut, gaping at the camera while Laura lay slumped in a hospital gown. Because of the baby and Laura having to stay home, the Shentons were always a bit poorer than the Grants — they rented, and the car was third-hand — but their lives were basically the same. Zoey was flower girl for both weddings, Laura and Mrs Grant were pregnant at the same time, and they lived five minutes away from each other – the Grants in Queens Park and Nathan's family in Bentley. Then, when Mr Grant became director of a small exploration company in the Pilbara, Bree's family got a house-and-land package in a new subdivision, pulling the families as far apart as they'd been for twenty years. It felt weird. Eventually, the Shentons followed like faithful dogs, building a house two streets away.

'Hop in the back with the girls there, sweetheart,' Mrs Grant said. 'We'll just be a second.'

Nathan could tell from the way she smiled that his mother was angry. He wondered if they'd been talking about Zoey, finally. His parents had told him not to tell Bree she was pregnant, and it'd been so hard it almost hurt.

Nathan yanked open the car door. Bree's younger sister sat in the very back, reading a Harry Potter book.

'Hi, Jessie.'

She barely looked up. ''Lo.'

Bree wrenched around from the front seat. 'Good morning, Gogo.'

'Good morning, Didi.'

Their other friend, Candice, was Pozzo. The three
had read *Waiting for Godot* all the way to the end,
unlike anyone else in their class.

'Your mum looks pissed off,' Bree said.

Nathan couldn't see Laura's face from his seat. 'Yep.'

'Isn't today her birthday?'

He nodded. Bree rolled her eyes. To them, forty
was an unreachable, embarrassing age. 'Remember my
mum's birthday?'

Nathan did. 'She got drunk.'

'And my dad.'

He blushed. There had been a huge fight between
Bree's parents right before they cut the cake, because
Mr Grant had taken a half-empty champagne bottle
out of his wife's hand and thrown it in their pool. Mrs
Grant had almost cried, saying how the Shentons had
bought it for her and she was just trying to share it with
her *friends*, for God's sake. Bree's dad, who seemed to
be over the argument as soon as his hand was empty,
told her not to spoil things. 'You're a mean man,' Mrs
Grant snivelled tearily, poking him in the chest. 'A
mean man.' But by the end of the night, Mr Grant's
fingers, wracked with whisky tremors, were back
vibrating against his wife's bum.

If there was one thing Nathan was never going to do, it was drink alcohol. The loss of control appalled him. How could you prevent people from laughing at you if you didn't even know what you were doing?

'Lame,' he said coolly.

'Heaps lame,' Bree agreed, turning back around.

The Grants could have been Nathan's parents, the amount of time he'd spent with them; secretly, he was glad they weren't. Mrs Grant liked to set rules, telling him to loosen his laces before he took off his shoes or to sit up straight at the dinner table – things Laura didn't care about – but then sometimes teased him, the way Bree did. Nathan didn't always know what to do when that happened. And Mr Grant, who was up north a lot, would appear from nowhere and fold his thick eyebrows as if he'd never seen Nathan before. He was once on their toilet when Mr Grant half-opened the door, making him scream. 'What the fu—' Mr Grant whispered, slamming it shut. Nathan got constipated whenever he thought of it.

A lock of Bree's hair snaked around the headrest to the back of her seat. It was shampoo-ad hair, a perfect shiny curl. Nathan couldn't stop staring. He didn't know how girls did it, with their flowery hairclips and brightly coloured pen sets and glossy mouths. They looked new every single morning.

Nathan and Bree had got married a million times in the backyard of the old house, but ever since his sister told them she was having a baby he'd become aware of Bree as a person, a *girl*, separate from himself, with her own interests and dreams and demands unfurling. They really could get married one day. The idea scared him the way the irregular stirrings between his legs scared him. He wanted to be Gogo and Didi forever.

Bree was looking at him in the rear-view mirror. 'Auditions today.'

'Auditions today,' he repeated. Ms Prior had chosen a series of scenes from *A Midsummer Night's Dream*. It was thrilling. Characters were in love with one another, characters were bewitched to love other characters, and donkeys and fairies clattered across the stage. They'd watched a film of it the week before, Ms Prior fast-forwarding to find the right parts, and the movement and colour made Nathan giddy. When they went outside into the light of lunchtime he felt drugged, in love with his friends. He took one in each arm and spun them, shrieking, and for a moment he wasn't worried it might give him an erection; in fact, he thought he understood why you might get one, how it might be kind of exciting.

'You'll be a fabulous Lysander.'

'You'll be an amazing Hermia.'

In the scene Ms Prior had picked, Lysander and Hermia kissed.

*

Nathan's first session on Fridays was Maths, which he hated, but at least his other friend Candice was in his class. Metal skewed her smile as he entered the room and Nathan felt lucky not to need braces. 'Gogo!'

'Hey, Pozzo.' He slid into the desk beside her.

'I'm *so* excited about auditions,' Candice said. She spoke carefully around the rubber bands, but there was still juice in her words. 'I'm freaking *out*.'

'You'll be great.'

Bree had claimed Candice, who'd gone to a different primary school and didn't know anyone, on the first day of high school. Bree decided to start fresh by snipping away extraneous friends, and while Nathan was pleased to be the sole survivor of the cut, it left him estranged from their old group. He'd worked hard to make those friends. Candice was Bree's peace offering; she brought her to him like a gift. They assigned her *Waiting for Godot*, and she reported back: loved it.

'But nothing happens,' Bree tested her.

Candice gave a single serious nod. 'Just like life.'

She was in.

At the beginning, Candice wasn't enrolled in the drama elective, but by the end of the first week she'd swapped out of food science, a highly prized option, to sit with Nathan and Bree in Ms Prior's class. The good thing about Candice was that she was eager to learn. At recess and lunch they played improvisation games, and Candice always listened when Bree suggested better choices. Since she lived further from school it was hard to hang out, but she started missing the earlier bus to walk home with Nathan and Bree. On the weekend she sometimes had them both sleep over, and Mrs Reyes made tall fizzy spiders and poured Coco Pops for breakfast. Nathan's and Bree's mothers didn't know; they would have been appalled at all that sugar.

Candice prodded him with a pencil. '*Nathan.*'

She was leaning at him, bunching her chest under her chin. He tried not to look. She continued, 'At the auditions today, I was thinking, you know, what if I went for Hermia instead of Helena?'

In the play, Hermia was the small, popular one, and Helena the unloved freak. Nathan squinted. 'But

Didi's going for Hermia.' This was Bree's idea. She was shorter than Candice.

'Yeah, I know.' Candice faced forward in her seat again and fiddled with her things, putting a folder on top of her textbook and then shifting it off again. 'I just thought, maybe *I* could go for it.'

'But Didi's going for it,' he said again.

The teacher called the class to attention. As she turned to the whiteboard and drew a parabola, Nathan started to panic. Candice was supposed to be Helena. The three of them had decided.

'Helena is crap,' Candice whispered, copying the graph into her notebook. 'Helena sucks.'

'She's a lead character.'

Candice exhaled dismissively. Spittle hit the point where her x and y axes intersected. 'She's the one nobody likes.'

'They like her in the end.'

'When they're all *drugged*.'

The teacher turned around. Candice clamped her lips shut over her braces and bent to her work. Furious with worry, Nathan drew a wobbly curve in his note-book. Bree was going to be really, really mad.

He sensed Candice's movements beside him. With each graph she methodically shuffled her page up out of the way of her breasts, which rested on the bottom half of the desk. Candice had the biggest chest in their year group: probably in the whole school. She wore extra-large boys' shirts and still the buttons strained and popped open, so she had special dispensation from the year coordinator to carry safety-pins in her pencil case.

At lunch the day before they'd rehearsed behind the science block: Candice as Helena, with Nathan as Demetrius, and Bree directing. Candice already knew her lines by heart. *'I am your spaniel,'* she exhorted, throwing herself at his feet. *'And, Demetrius, the more you beat me I will fawn on you.'*

Bree stood in front of them. Over her shoulder a group of older boys gathered, nudging one another and making faces. Candice looked down at her chest, then jerked up.

Their director frowned. 'Hands and knees, Pozzo.'

Behind her, the boys burst out laughing. Candice faltered. 'Ah…'

'Use me but as your spaniel,' Bree prompted.

'Use…'

Nathan tried to interrupt. 'Didi—'

'*Use me but as your spaniel!*'

The boys were exaggerating their laughter now, falling over each other to be most obnoxious. '*Spaniel!*' one of them hooted. 'Spaniel! Spaniel!'

Finally realising, Bree turned and looked for a second, then settled back. 'Ignore them.'

Candice fixed her gaze on Nathan. The corners of her mouth and eyes were wet. He could see right down her shirt. '*Use me but as your spaniel.*'

At the desk beside him, Candice swallowed. He could see the tops of her breasts quiver as her arm bumped them. The sums blurred on the board. He wanted to tell her she was beautiful and that those guys yesterday were dickheads. But you didn't just *say* that.

In a play, maybe you could.

'Okay,' he whispered, eyes facing forwards in case the teacher looked around again.

'What?'

'Go for Hermia. If you really want to.'

He heard spit move in her mouth as she smiled.

*

One summer when Nathan was four or five, his mum's side of the family had a reunion. His great-grandmother, Laura's grandmother, was ninety-five, and they hadn't wanted to wait in case she didn't make one hundred. Nathan's great aunts went down to the foreshore on a Sunday morning and staked out an area with folding chairs. At lunchtime the entire bloodline had a barbecue by the river, four generations with Great-Nan at the top.

Nathan's family drove down mid-morning. His parents sat in the front of the Mazda, talking softly below the roar of warmth from the air vents, hands rolling over one another on the centre console. They parked and carried their Eskies past the Mends Street Jetty and play equipment to where Laura's family had camped. Nathan remembers the heat stinging his forearms and the tightness of the hat Rob kept wedging down on his head, and sausages in white bread served by an uncle. Great-Nan sat under the coolest tree they could find, waving a birthday card in her face for the breeze, frowning. Laura went to put Nathan on her lap and Great-Nan held a hand up to stop her. 'It's too hot,' she groaned, peeling the damp cotton from her skirt off her thighs. Great-Nan was fat and wore eight-dollar floral sundresses from Best & Less, even on her birthday.

Zoey led him off with the other cousins, who were languishing under another tree, sucking on home-made icy poles and trying to work out whose shoes were the best. Zoey stopped them before they got to her – the Shenton kids' thongs were two dollars from the supermarket and had a strap at the back so they didn't come off – and changed the subject. 'Nathan,' she said, spinning him to face the rest of the group, 'Play Great-Nan.'

'What?'

'Play Great-Nan.'

Nathan felt even hotter, a burn of embarrassment spreading across his cheeks and forehead. The cousins were looking and he was thrilled by their attention, but it was frightening because he didn't know what to do. They could turn at any second.

The night before, during dinner, Laura had told them about the upcoming picnic. 'It's for your great-grandmother.'

He didn't know who that was. Laura tried to explain. 'You know, my grandma. Nanny's mother.'

'Is she the one –' Nathan put his arms out in a circle to demonstrate weight, then smoothed an imaginary dress over his knees. 'She calls us kidlets.' He mimicked her deep voice. '*Hello, kidlets; hello, kidlets.*'

Zoey snorted. Rob smirked, but tried not to. 'That's a bit rude,' he said, to cover it up. 'Don't do it in front of Great-Nan.'

The cousins were waiting. Nathan looked around to make sure his parents and Great-Nan weren't watching, then pooched his stomach out as far as it would go. 'Kidlets!' he boomed. 'Look at all these kidlets running around.'

A couple of cousins giggled. Zoey was grinning. Nathan drew courage and began to flop a hand in front of his face. 'It's too hot! I'm sweating like a pig, kidlets!' He lifted the other arm and fanned his armpit madly. The rest of the cousins were smiling and laughing now. A few joined in, holding their imaginary guts like full-term pregnancies and waddling around the grass. One broke into an impression of Great-Uncle Pete, Great-Nan's oldest son, who snorted heavily between sentences and rubbed his palms together. Others began to offer up different uncles and aunts, parents, even their own brothers and sisters.

Zoey gave him a kiss. Nathan beamed and rubbed his finger under the rim of his hat where it itched, the attention fizzing in his veins. For a few moments he'd been another person, said the things that person would say, and the crowd had given their approval; they wanted to be like him.

Later, he realised what he'd done – mocked his great-grandma, an old lady who was just fat and hot – to get the others to like him, and he felt uneasy. But his dad had only told him not to do it in front of Great-Nan. No-one was hurt by it, not really.

Laura said the barbecue hadn't happened – not the way Nathan thought it did. 'You were two years old at that reunion,' she told him when he brought it up. 'I remember I had to change your nappy in the boot of the car.'

'It was for Great-Nan's birthday.'

'It wasn't her birthday.' The two of them and Zoey were picking out new furniture; they'd just signed up to build the house, and all of a sudden Laura couldn't stand the stuff they lived with. She ran her palm over a wooden desk for Nathan's room, checking the dimen-sions on the label. 'It was stinking hot, and Great-Nan's birthday was in May.'

'I thought she was ninety-five.'

Laura tested the drawers. 'She might have been ninety-five, but it wasn't her birthday. And if she was ninety-five, you definitely weren't more than three.'

Nathan turned to Zoey. She was still living at home then, though she was getting more private. But it was hard to spark her memory when he couldn't say, in front of Laura, what they'd been doing in the little group of cousins. 'Zo?'

Zoey shrugged. 'Maybe.'

But Nathan was sure he was right.

He also remembered sitting on Laura's lap at his sister's Christmas assembly, when Zoey was one of the three Wise Men. Once the doll-baby Jesus was born she stepped onstage, wearing a dressing-gown and tea towel, and held out her gift. 'I bring frankincense,' she announced, pronouncing the word clearly, and the girl playing Mary took it. Zoey hadn't had to guess; she knew just what to say. The show finished and Nathan watched, thrilled, as the Wise Men and Joseph and Mary and the innkeeper and all the animals formed a line and bent towards to the audience, who clapped and whistled. As they packed up to go, Nathan asked Laura, 'Will I do that at big school?'

'That's right, mate,' she said. 'You might even get to be Joseph.'

Nathan hasn't asked Laura about this conversation in case she tells him it never happened, or that it wasn't like that. He knows how it felt to see his sister bow to happy, steady applause. All Zoey had to do was pretend.

*

At recess, Candice's suggestion that she could audition for Hermia went pretty much as Nathan expected. 'You're too tall,' Bree objected. 'Anyway, we've already organised it. You know all Helena's lines.'

'I'm sick of being the ugly one.'

Bree's face curled. 'It's a play.'

'I don't care. It says something about me.'

Bree turned to Nathan. 'Gogo, tell her it's a *play*.'

'Yeah, it is a play,' Candice shouted. 'That's why it's *important!*'

Bree shook her head. 'You're crazy. You're crazy.'

Nathan thought back to when he had male friends.

His next two classes were Phys. Ed., then drama. The game that Friday was soccer and Nathan was forced into a stinking red bib from a tub in the sports shed. He stood in his team's defensive half, near the goal but not near enough to help, hunching his shoulders and checking his watch. At one point the ball came dangerously close and he reared back, remembering at the final moment to put out a foot like he was doing something.

When they were let go, there was the change room to cope with: a windowless box lined with wooden benches, no curtains, no privacy, and only three loos and two showers for thirty boys. The showers were for after-school sports, not Phys. Ed., and the water was shut off, so if you went in there to change everyone knew you were hiding and decided you had a small dick. They said this even though they couldn't see it, which was why you might hide in the first place. Usually Nathan lined up outside the toilets, pretending to need a wee and changing while he was in there, but today there was already a queue and he didn't want to be late for the auditions. He found a dark corner of the change room and turned his back on the others. In a hurry, he tucked his thumbs into the waistband of his shorts and pushed them down.

The tiniest, briefest millimetre of his jocks caught in the material. He noticed practically immediately and adjusted them, making sure no hint of a private part had defied the elastic. Only a sliver of bum crack had met the light, only for a second in a loud, seething room, but it didn't matter. Someone shouted, 'Nice arse!'

The blood in Nathan's body shot to his face. His penis cowered. Opening, again, was the bullying window for him to slip into, avoiding the edges like a game of Operation: be careful-careful so he didn't moon them again. He stretched the waistband out wide before bending over and pushing his shorts to his ankles. He kicked them away, praying his white Rios were clean of skid-marks.

Two other boys, both shirtless, moved closer to him. One had dark, straight chest hair reaching from his clavicle up his neck, forming a bed for a slim gold chain. He was deep into puberty like a forest. The other was wiry but muscled from sport. He was the one who'd asked Mr Miller if the guy in *Tony's Story* was going to stay back and masturbate. 'Tippy-toes, tippy-toes,' he said in a high voice, and the other boy snuffled like a cartoon pig.

If Nathan had known what to say, he would've said it. Instead he found his regular pants in his schoolbag and stepped into them. Once they were fastened, the worst would be over.

'Wait,' the muscled one interrupted. 'Did you just do your button up before the zip?'

A few others in the change room were looking as they dressed, paying attention just in case.

'Yeah?' Nathan asked.

The muscled one started laughing. Hairy Neck looked across at his friend and smiled, but didn't seem to get the joke. Nathan didn't, either. Keeping his ear on the other two so they couldn't say he was ignoring them, he closed the zip.

The kid finished laughing. 'Der, you zip *before* you button.' He nudged his mate. 'Right?'

'Definitely,' Hairy Neck said, his grin widening. His lips were scaly and cratering in the corners, and he stank of grass and sweat. Nathan didn't understand why some people got a pass and others didn't.

The two of them started laughing again, and Nathan hoped this was the end of their show. What else could they say? He shifted his gaze to the wall, which at the start of the year had been covered in drawings of penises and crude messages. After his first class, as Nathan was packing his dirty clothes back into his bag, he'd realised the spot had been marked with a wobbly arrow and the announcement, in thick black Texta, that *cassie isnt a virgin*!

During the winter holidays they'd covered up the graffiti with thick khaki paint. Term started and the others hunted for their favourites, whining 'Ripped off!' when they couldn't find anything. At assembly the principal told them they were expected to treat school property with respect, but it didn't last. There were already new willies on the walls, bigger and hairier than ever before.

Hearing the laughter of Muscles and Hairy Neck die away, Nathan took a chance and stripped off his polo shirt. No-one commented on his bare, shapeless chest. He was almost free.

'Pick up the pace, boys,' Mr Miller shouted from the doorway. He was the one who made the class late and then wandered around as they changed, yelling.

'Hey, Mr Miller,' Muscles called. He was still topless. 'When you do your pants up, do you do the button first, or the zip?'

Nathan stopped.

'Wha' a' you on about, Leo?' the teacher drawled, smirking. Muscles – Leo – had been Nathan's team's goalie in the game they just played, saving five shots and keeping the Bibs and Shirts to a scoreless draw. Mr Miller loved him.

'Don't you think it's weird to do the button up first?' the hairy-chested one chimed in. 'Wouldn't you be more likely to have an *accident* –' Leo snorted, and Hairy Neck nudged him, '– that way?'

Mr Miller looked at Nathan, who was putting on his dress shirt one shaking sleeve at a time. 'You three ge' a move on,' he said indulgently, as if Nathan, who'd made sure not to touch the ball today, was in on a joke with the two best players in class. 'There's another group comin' in.'

When Mr Miller left, Leo leaned in. 'Don't wanna zip your dick, do ya?'

Nathan stared hard at the wall until they were gone, knowing what would be there next week. A sharp little drawing of himself, willy drooping from his wide-open fly, on the new green paint.

*

When he finally got to drama class Candice and Bree were sitting on opposite sides of the room. Under the window Candice mouthed along with her script, throwing a hand against her chest and then clenching it into a fist. Nathan wanted to sit with her but he'd have to walk past Bree. He imagined her slow-motion reaction if he did that: hair standing on end, fire erupting in the background. The end of the world.

'Gogo,' Bree called, patting the seat next to her.

He sat. 'Why's Pozzo over there?'

Bree's face sharpened. She tipped her corkscrew hair forward. 'Don't ask.'

Auditions for the male characters went first. Nathan did win the part of Lysander, though it was a very unsatisfactory experience. There were only five boys who took drama in the first place and the other four wanted to be Bottom. In the end Ms Prior had to forcibly assign the main roles and Nathan was given Lysander without even trying, though he insisted on reading a soliloquy since he'd practised and everything. *'I am, my lord, as well derived as he, as well possessed. My love is more than his, my fortunes every way as fairly ranked—'*

'Great, great.'

Returning to his chair Nathan tried to catch someone's eye for a sympathetic frown, but Bree's attention was fixed on Candice, who never looked up from her book.

In the end neither of his friends got the part opposite him. Two-thirds of the girls wanted to be the delicate, dainty, over-loved Hermia, and the role was given to a delicate, dainty, over-loved girl from the popular group, who had a plump mouth and belly-button ring. Muttering dejectedly, the Hermias left the stage and the Helenas took their place. Candice joined the end of this queue as well.

Bree sat back next to him. 'What a bitch.'

His heart seized. 'Who?'

'Ms Prior. She doesn't know anything.'

A couple of Helenas waggled petulantly across the room and Ms Prior wrote in her book, stifling a yawn. Candice stood at the edge of the stage, big chest rising and falling. It was her turn.

She strode out of the line, stopped at the invisible X, and paused. When her eyes met Nathan's he gave her an encouraging smile.

Abruptly she changed, throwing herself on all fours and exposing the soft skin inside her wrists. Along her shirt, pins tugged and glinted under the lights. '*Use me but as your spaniel,*' she pleaded to nobody, her voice deeper than usual. She pushed a knee from her skirt and leaned into it. It was 'sexy', Nathan realised, and his intestines rolled with distress. He thought of Candice's sisters perfuming the Reyes' kitchen on a Saturday night, of Mrs Grant in a silk dressing-gown, offering him cheese on toast and asking what kind of man he wanted to be. Nathan, the cheese waxy in his mouth, hadn't known you could choose.

Candice finished her speech and fell still, the bewitchment over. Behind her, the other girls exchanged looks in a Mexican wave of judgement. Ms Prior hadn't made any notes.

'Oh my God,' Bree whispered.

Ms Prior finally interrupted the muttering. 'Thank you, Candice.'

His friend's face was bright red. She returned to the queue and stared out at nothing, bunched fists slowly drawing together at her thighs.

When Ms Prior gave the part to someone else, Candice nodded and took her seat carefully, as if she had an injury to protect. She didn't go for any of the other roles and nodded mutely when Ms Prior gave her one at random. Nathan looked at Bree, who had her arms crossed and an unreadable look on her face, and hoped she wouldn't say anything. By the time the bell had finished ringing for lunch, Candice was gone.

*

Nathan would never have even met Candice if, instead of the nearby private school, he'd been able to go to his first choice: the special performing arts college in the city, whose students went on to WAAPA and NIDA and probably those educational videos, too. If he'd gone there, Nathan would've had real competition for the role of Lysander and genuine approval when he auditioned so flawlessly. He'd have more than two friends, and no-one hassling him over how he fastened his pants.

The year before, both Nathan and Bree had tried to get in. Seeing the thousand-seat theatre where auditions were held, Nathan had wanted to cry with longing. He imagined nesting in the orchestra pit, feeding himself from the vending machines, laying washing out to dry on the red velvet chairs. Home.

There was a long list of kids who also wanted to go there, so three at a time they waited in the green room – which wasn't green, but Nathan pretended not to be surprised – while the rest lined up in alphabetical order in a hallway. Bree was ahead of him, talking to a girl Nathan recognised from a Saturday TV show about crime-solving twins in Fremantle. She was the sensible twin while her brother was spontaneous: a trait that threatened to ruin all of their investigations, but in the end always led to them catching the crook.

After an hour he was let into the room. The boy at the other end of the couch was looking at the ceiling and muttering, and frowned when Nathan leaned forward to watch. Between them was a girl with long golden limbs who sat very still.

Someone opened the door and beckoned the other boy, who strode out. As soon as he was gone the golden girl spoke. 'Do you know who that was?'

'Um.' Nathan tried to remember the name that was called. 'No?'

She rolled her eyes. Nathan was sure she couldn't be twelve, like him. Her voice was high and tight. 'He was the Boy in *Waiting for Godot* when they did it at His Majesty's?'

'What's that?'

She shook her head. After someone came in to get her Nathan tried to remember the name of the play she'd mentioned: *Waiting for Goddoh.*

Two weeks after the audition, Nathan answered the Shentons' phone in the old house. 'Hello, Nathan speaking.'

'Hello, Nathan Speaking.' Mrs Grant's regular joke. 'How are you, bubs?'

'Um, Mum's not here—'

'I'm actually not calling for Laura. I'm after you.'

His stomach sank. 'Oh.'

Bree had got a letter from the drama school and wouldn't leave her room, Mrs Grant told him. Would he come over and talk to her?

Twenty minutes later Mrs Grant honked from the street. Nathan told Zoey where he was going and went outside, stopping on the way to check their letterbox. Folded into a supermarket catalogue was a white envelope addressed to him. He tore it open with excitement. Under his name, in bold capitals, was the word CONGRATULATIONS.

Mrs Grant spoke to him from the front seat but Nathan wasn't listening. *Congratulations!* He stared out of the window at the passing cars, a procession just for him. He was back on that big stage, bending into a deep bow, the hum of the highway a throng of applause. He was going to be so popular.

Bree didn't talk until they were in her room, where she flung herself on the bed beside her own letter. 'I can't *believe* it.'

Nathan bent over her shoulder. *We regret to advise...* 'Oh, Bree.'

She sat up again, agitated. 'It's so unfair.' Her eyes were red and dry. She picked at the corner of her pillowcase, then flung it against the bedhead. 'I'm going to get an agent anyway. I asked the girl from *Crime Catchers* to email me.'

'An agent?'

Bree frowned, mistaking his envy for sarcasm. 'Did you get a no, too?'

Nathan was hurt. He pulled the letter from his pocket. 'I got in.'

Her eyes widening, Bree snatched it. 'A second audition? Not fair.'

'What?' Nathan took it back. 'No, it says "congratulations"—'

'On getting a second audition.' She jabbed at the first paragraph. 'There's a time and date and stuff. It's next week.'

'Oh.'

He had a bad thought: *At least they think I'm better than you.*

She seemed to sense it. Twisting from her spot on the bed, she latched two hands to his elbow. 'Are you going to do it?'

'Why wouldn't I?'

She let go. 'Well, if you get in, that's great, but you won't know anyone. You won't have any friends.'

Nathan thought again of the slim-limbed girl in the audition room, and the guy who talked to himself and was in *Waiting for Goddoh*. The freckled twin from the crime show, looking bored.

Bree rubbed the skin below one eye. He couldn't tell if she'd actually been crying. 'But totally do what you want.'

Nathan didn't know what that was. He folded the letter and put it back in his pocket. Where was his home, without Bree? He lay down next to her.

'Hey,' she said. 'Maybe we'll get the same agent.'

'Maybe.'

She put her hand on his shoulder. He didn't really want it there, but he couldn't ask her to move. They lay like that and listened to the late autumn wind rushing down the main street of the estate where the Grants lived. Soon Nathan would live there, too.

*

When the final bell rang the day of the auditions, Bree was waiting outside his class. '*Finally,*' she groaned, pulling him from the rush. 'Come on, let's go.'

'Where's Candice?'

Bree was yanking his arm just about out of its socket as she led him around the perimeter of the school. Usually the three of them met in the main quadrangle.

'We should at least tell her we're leaving.'

'She'll be gone by now anyway.'

No she wouldn't. He knew Candice: she would wait for ages.

They trudged across the oval without talking. Older kids shot past on bikes, gouging out hunks of soft earth with their tyres. Nathan skipped out of the way as one twisted his wheel at a dirt clod like he was kicking a soccer ball.

'Poof,' the boy snorted as he cycled away, arse held high in the air.

Nathan set the muscles in his arms and legs, pretending he hadn't heard.

Bree bumped him self-consciously, both hands pulling at the straps of her backpack. She stopped in some shade.

'What?' he asked.

She dug a foot into the soil to draw out the pause. He remembered Candice on her knees, looking up at him. *If you beat me, I will fawn on you.* Nathan smelled coconut hair wax as his scalp began to sweat.

'I think my parents are going to get a divorce,' she said.

Nathan's eyebrows lifted. He remembered Mrs Grant standing outside the car that morning, speaking to Laura, not letting him hear. That was unusual. Bree's mother didn't keep secrets, she'd tell anybody anything: Milton was spending all their money up north, she never knew what he was up to, he never talked to her. Her voice was cheerful, like she was poking fun at herself. *'I thought the time apart would make us closer, but look what happens.'* When Mr Grant came home, she kept going, as if he were deaf. *'You'd think I'd get a little help, but it's like I've got three kids instead of two!'* she told nobody, smiling enormously. Mr Grant walked through the house with his shoulders hunched and his face like a dirty drain, fending her off the same way Nathan did with bullies. Surely they'd stopped loving one another a long time ago.

'Who said?' Nathan asked.

Bree pushed off the tree she'd been leaning against and stalked across to the footpath. He hurried to catch up.

'Dad wants to move up near the mine, but Mum doesn't.'

'Okay.'

'He reckons he isn't even going to your mum's party tonight.'

'Oh.' It would be kind of good not having Mr Grant there, shuffling in the shadows and rolling his shoulders like he was itchy, his hands smelling of hot metal.

It was a warm day for September. The heat was making Nathan feel a little sick. The woodchips between the path and the kerb stank of dirt, and flies whined in the heavy air. He wished they were at Candice's, Mrs Reyes serving them tall buzzing glasses of Coke.

'If they get a divorce I'll have to move anyway,' Bree said. She sounded almost excited about it. 'Mum said. Neither of them can afford the new house on their own.'

Nathan didn't respond.

She said, in a dancing voice, 'You'd miss me if I moved!'

'But you'd still go to the same school.'

He could tell Bree was spoiling for a fight. She had been ever since recess, when Candice wouldn't do as she was told.

'What if I didn't?'

He began to walk faster. Soon she was tripping over her own ankles trying to catch up. 'Hey. Wouldn't you miss me?'

'Shut up.'

They were silent for the rest of the walk. The sun cut through Nathan's shirt, making him sweat under the heavy straps of his schoolbag. The cars passing were loud and close and he just wanted to get away from Bree for a while.

Finally, there was his driveway. 'Okay, well, I have to go—'

'Wait.'

'What?'

She was flushed by the walk and spat a curl out of her mouth. 'I don't want to move away.'

He groaned. 'You won't.'

She stopped and crossed her arms. When she looked up her eyes were funny. 'I can't leave now, Gogo.'

'Why?'

Bree's throat moved as she swallowed. 'Because I *like* you.'

The road here was quiet. Nathan felt two beads of sweat, one from each armpit, fall inside his shirt. Bree's lips were quivering around her half-smile, like she was holding a pose at the end of a scene. She had the script and he didn't. He wondered if she'd be doing this if Ms Prior had let her be Hermia.

After a moment, she stepped back and put her hands on her hips. Whatever the script was, he hadn't followed it.

'Candice likes you too,' she added.

Nathan's head jerked. 'Are you serious?'

'Don't tell her I told you. She'd be really mad.'

It was too warm for him. 'I have to go,' he said again.

Bree shrugged. 'Well, I might not come tonight. I might stay with my dad.'

'Alright.'

'Unless you want me to come.'

'Well, you're invited. And so's your dad.'

She played with a curl. 'Whatever.'

Her eyes were a challenge, but he wasn't sure to what. He went into the house and it was nice and cool. He called out tentatively from the entryway but no-one answered.

Nathan dropped his schoolbag and lay on the cold tiles, spreading his arms and legs out. After a moment his hands went to his chest. He thought of Candice's breasts and of her pose in Drama that day. Her need to be sexy, instead of ugly. *Candice likes you, too.* That might not be true, since Bree had been crazy today. Still, he repeated it to himself, imagining Candice in a crouch and seeing the dark, miraculous line of her cleavage. It felt like he was lying on his pants wrong, the material pulling in the front, but he wasn't. He enjoyed the discomfort for a moment. Then he remembered how he and Bree had left school before Candice could find them, and he felt as bad as she must have, walking down to the bus stop, alone.

*

Nathan's job was to open big bags of chips and pour them into bowls, and to unstack the tubes of plastic cups so people could get to them more easily. As he worked, his father lifted bottles of alcohol from cartons, lining them up on the trestle table in height order. Rob had already moved the CD player onto the patio and Bruce Springsteen played, Laura's favourite. She came out of the house in a small silver dress, holding a cup of liquid that looked like Coke but smelled like house cleaner. Nathan had never seen so much of his mother's legs before and couldn't help but look. She wore chunky high heels. Veins strained on the tops of her feet.

You're going to be a grandma, Nathan realised, but was smart enough not to say. Laura, drinking, rearranged the chip bowls.

Mrs Grant and Jessie arrived, with Milton and Bree behind them – a visual representation of how much each person wanted to come to the party. When Nathan opened the door, Mrs Grant lifted an arm and hooted, 'Let's get this party started!' Her dress was shorter than Laura's, and red.

No-one responded. Nathan wondered if Mr and Mrs Grant were indeed getting a divorce, or whether Bree was just being dramatic. Did divorcing people go to parties together? Their faces gave nothing away; they looked how they always did – Mr Grant grumpy, Mrs Grant exhilarated.

Jessie waved her book at Nathan and went through to the games room. Bree followed, pausing halfway to give him a look full of feeling. They were in a fight. Nathan's guts curdled. 'Aren't you going to say hello?'

Mrs Grant called after her daughter. She said to Nathan, 'Women, hey?'

Nathan went to his room and kicked his director's chair so it collapsed on the floor, then went back out to the patio.

His father turned up the stereo for 'Born to Run'. His mother's friends came up and patted his shoulders and the top of his head, telling him how proud Laura must be. One woman explained in detail how much worse her son was compared to him; he was fifteen and had dropped out of school, said he was going to do an apprenticeship but wasn't. 'What are you going to be, Nathan?' the lady asked, her arm around his waist. 'Something professional? An accountant, a lawyer?'

'I want to be an actor,' Nathan told her.

Her grip on him slackened. 'Oh, sweetie,' she said, kindly. 'That's silly.'

He wanted to go and talk to Bree but he also didn't want to give her the satisfaction. He sat in a plastic chair next to his grandmother and drank lemonade, watching Mr Grant pace around the lawn like a lion in a cage.

His father came up and put a hand on the back of his neck. 'Natey,' he said, a nickname he used when he was emotional. 'Let's go inside.'

Rob led him through the kitchen, past the glass doors to the games room where Bree stared out angrily, and down the hallway. At the front of the house was a formal lounge room; they hadn't had one before, and Laura filled it with white leather furniture and told Nathan he must never go in there. (What kind of mess did she think he'd make?) There stood Zoey, bare feet digging into the carpet, her eyes made up in black liner. The boyfriend that their parents had met twice and Nathan only once wasn't there.

'Zo!' he shouted and lunged at his sister. She hugged him back with the force of five missed months and he realised there was no belly between them. 'Zo, what happened?'

When she pulled back, the makeup was slipping from under her eyes. She wiped the smudges off with her thumbs and shook her head.

'Are you moving back in?' he asked.

Rob reached out like a father in a sitcom and put his hands on his children's shoulders. His breath was whisky. 'There's a lot to talk about,' he said. 'We're going to take some time this weekend and try to figure it out.'

'Are you coming out to the party?'

His dad squeezed hard enough to make him wince. Zoey grimaced as well.

'I don't think Mum wants me to,' she said.

'She's very hurt,' Rob explained for them. 'Now she's been drinking, you know it won't go well, love.'

Zoey didn't respond. When no-one was speaking they could hear the muffle of chatter and music in the backyard.

Nathan's sister frowned. 'Are you playing "Glory Days"? Really?'

Their dad shrugged. Nathan didn't understand Zoey's smirk.

'Well, anyway,' she said, and took a step back, out of Rob's grasp. As his hand fell, hers rose to her stomach for a moment. 'I just wanted to see you, little dude. What's up?'

'I'm going to be Lysander in a play,' Nathan said. Rob was still holding his shoulder. Through his shirt the grip felt damp.

'Cool,' Zoey said. 'Who is that?'

Nathan was going to explain, but instead he said, 'Do you remember the assembly you did in primary school, when you played one of the Wise Men? You gave the baby frankincense.'

His sister smiled.

'That really made me want to be an actor.'

To his surprise, Zoey said, 'I know.'

'You do?'

'You told me when I came home from school. "*I want to do that too, Zo-Zo.*" You made me play it out with you for weeks.'

When Nathan went back outside someone was sitting in his chair, so he got a handful of chips and roamed around the backyard. This party was nothing like he'd imagined. He'd wanted so much to play adults with Bree before she bullied Candice and told Nathan she liked him. Now she was presiding over the inside of the house like some bitch queen. If she'd stayed home like she promised he could've gone into the games room with Jessie and read Harry Potter books until all the adults died of drunkenness.

Rob changed the CD in the middle of 'Dancing in the Dark'. Nathan's mother's protests came from a dark corner of the garden. He walked over to see what she was doing.

A new song started: 'Somebody to Love', by Queen. Laura stood under the washing line with Mr Grant, who had his eyes shut and was pinching his nose, high and tight, like it'd been bleeding. She was rubbing his back and whispering.

Should Nathan care that Bree's parents were supposed to be getting a divorce, that they'd be moving away, again leaving the Shentons behind? If Mr and Mrs Grant broke up, would Rob and Laura, out of a lack of imagination, do the same thing?

Laura saw him. 'Nathan, sweetie,' she said. 'Come here.'

Nathan thought of his big sister and her empty belly, the tears smudged under her eyes. Zoey never cried. She'd got in her car and driven back to wherever she was living now.

'Come home soon,' he'd said, as he hugged her goodbye. 'I don't like being the only kid in this house.'

'You'll be grown up soon enough,' Zoey said.

Grown up, with the armpits and voice and problems of Tony. This afternoon he'd got excited, thinking about Candice. *'What kind of man are you going to be?'* Mrs Grant had asked him once, her eyes gleaming, her breath bad.

'Nathan?' Laura called. 'Are you listening to me?'

He turned around and went back inside.

*

It was cold in the park. Cycling there as fast as he could Nathan's thighs had burned, warming his whole body, but now the hairs stood up from their tiny mounds and he shivered. Candice had picked up the phone almost on the first ring, as if she'd been waiting, and immediately agreed to meet him. He'd barely even said hello.

On the way out, Bree and her dad were standing in the driveway having an argument. She stopped when she saw Nathan. 'Where are you going?'

'Won't be long,' he replied, and jumped on his bike.

Now, trembling in the breeze, Nathan tucked his hands deeper into his armpits and started wandering around the playground. He was more nervous than chilly, pacing across the soft padding that stopped kids breaking their coccyx as they came off the slide. He knelt to test the sponginess with his hand. When he stood up again Candice still wasn't there, so he sat the wrong way in the belted baby swing, his bum cheeks in the leg-holes and the back-strap fastened over his crotch. It pulled too tight when he tried to swing, the metal hook cutting into his pubic bone, so he moved to the regular one. Just as he sat down Candice appeared, steering her bike across the grass.

All of a sudden, Nathan was scared. 'Hi.'

'Hi.'

'I didn't think you were coming.'

She dropped her bike and stood by a light-pole, one arm twisted around it, face lowered towards her left shoulder. 'I had to wait until my parents went to bed,' she explained. Her dark hair was out of its ponytail. 'You went home without me.'

'Sorry,' he said.

Candice kept looking down.

'I wanted to wait.'

She shrugged. Nathan spun in his seat, twisting the chains around themselves. They squeaked. After a while, Candice's chin twitched like she was going to look at him, but she didn't.

'How's the party?'

He shrugged. 'A bunch of adults drinking. Boring.'

'Was Bree there?'

He thought it was better not to answer. 'Zoey came for a bit,' he said.

'Is she going to move back?'

Nathan was relieved that he'd listened to his mother and kept quiet about his sister's baby. He could imagine all the crap they'd spout about being an uncle, both girls desperate to talk about the niece or nephew, fighting for a chance to see it when it was born. Now he wouldn't have to explain. 'I'm not sure. Maybe.'

Nathan dug the tip of his sneaker into the squishy, fake ground. 'I'm sorry you don't get to be Helena,' he said.

'I didn't want to be Helena. I wanted to be Hermia.'

'Right.'

'And Bree didn't get to be Hermia, either.'

Nathan pushed his toes until they ached.

Candice was still wound around the pole, but she finally looked at him. Hair hung in her eyes. 'So your first kiss will be with a girl from the popular group.'

He hadn't thought of that. 'I guess so,' he muttered.

She shrugged for a second time.

He wasn't sure what to say next so he started to swing, just a bit at first but then, when Candice blinked at him and there was a blooming *whoosh* in his stomach, higher and higher, so he could feel the tug in his legs as he pushed himself. The air on his skin was nice now. Maybe he could still salvage this day.

Candice let go of the pole and stepped towards him. 'That looks fun.'

'Whee,' he responded nervously, missing a beat and kicking his legs against himself.

She put her shoulders back and walked to the baby swing. She tried to sit, but her hips wouldn't fit. 'It's too small.'

He reversed his kicking so his arc steadily shortened. When the swing stopped Nathan took his hands off the chains, releasing the spicy scent of metal. 'Want a go?'

Candice resumed the look she'd had in drama that morning: tilted chin, big eyes, strange lips. He felt his stomach swing again.

'We could go together,' she suggested.

He wasn't sure what that meant.

With a deep breath she lifted her right leg and threaded it between his waist and the metal chain, her inner thigh resting half on the rubber seat and half against his left hip. Taking the chains in both hands, she hoisted herself off the ground and eased her other leg through the same space on Nathan's right side, pushing her hips forward to get her balance. The swing bucked and parts of Candice pushed against him. When everything settled, she was sitting in his lap, their faces centimetres apart.

Nathan was very aware of his breathing. Night air and anticipation sparked his asthma and he tried not to wheeze. The more he noticed his breaths the more they seemed out of sync, the inhalations long and ragged, the exhalations truncated with worry about the smell. He noticed they were making eye contact and looked down. There were her breasts, closer to him than ever.

Her thighs tightened against his hips and he realised she was pointing her toes, trying to get purchase against the soft ground. Her centre of gravity was thrown forward so their chests touched. Nathan gasped.

'Did I hurt you?' she asked.

He wished he had some Ventolin. 'No. Pozzo—'

'Can you not call me that anymore?'

Nathan couldn't answer.

Candice scrabbled a bit against the ground and then leaned back into the swing, pushing her legs out again and then tucking them back, pushing them out and tucking them back. Every time she did the mystery point at the top of her thighs came a tiny bit closer to his own.

'So, Hippolyta,' he said. 'That's a good role.'

Together they were heavy and inert, and the swing rocked reluctantly.

'What?'

'It's small but good.'

She kept rocking. He swallowed.

'I could call you that instead.' After a second, Nathan felt the muscles in her thighs slacken and her warm weight slide backwards a little.

'What?' she said again.

'Hippolyta. And I'll be Lysander. We could call – it could be names for just each other.'

Candice's bum was on his knees now, breasts rearing away from him. The swinging had stopped and he was tilting forward.

'You don't always have to be acting,' she told him. Her eyes were intense. 'I'm a real person, you know.'

He knew the kind of thing he should say, *I'm sorry* or *I know*, except that wouldn't turn things around fast enough; it had to be *You're really pretty* or a suave, whispered *Come here*. Then the kiss, because why else would she have put her face so close to his, unless she thought he'd kiss her? Why else did she want to be Hermia?

He couldn't do it. His asthma, his panic, he'd cough in her face, clash teeth, bite her tongue, get stuck in those braces.

Faces spun around, laughing.

She had a big blackhead on her chin. He fixed his eyes on it. 'Did you know Didi's parents are getting a divorce?'

Candice twisted angrily, yanking her leg out and tipping dangerously after it. Her right thigh was hot against his crotch and he winced. She couldn't get her foot underneath her and finally slid off, grabbing at his shirt and pulling him over her onto the ground. One of his knees stung as the skin grated off. Splayed on the asphalt, Candice's shinbone pressing against his penis and his face in her armpit, Nathan didn't know his line. He couldn't stop the moment from ending. *Treat me as your spaniel*, he should have said. *If you beat me, I will fawn on you.*

Killer

As soon as Teagan gets home from work her brother makes her come see the dog he's chained to the bent Hills Hoist outside the kitchen.

'Guy who had her called her Cassie,' Skyler says. The sliding door screams open and the dog steps towards them, alert. 'Named after his ex, 'cause he said she was a bitch.'

He laughs and Teagan sees spaces in the back of his mouth where silver and black teeth have fallen out. 'That's a nice name,' she says.

They stop a couple of metres back from the dog. She is tense, the hair along her spine fanned in warning. Her chest and shoulders are as broad as a human's, muscles pulsing like a bag of snakes. 'I'm'unna call her Killer instead.'

As if to demonstrate, the dog pushes into the brace of her collar and bares her teeth, massive paws digging for purchase in the earth. Teagan's hand floats to her bare throat. 'Why'd the owner get rid of her?'

Skyler thrusts his forearm into her waist and the sudden movement makes the dog growl – a deep rumble like a truck taking the hill in low gear.

'I *said*, she reminds him of his ex.'

Teagan turns so she is side on to Killer, trying to look less like a threat. It works; the dog sits back on the grass, her dense snout still raised in suspicion. 'She's very handsome.'

'We need some protection round here. Gonna train her to bite.'

Teagan nods carefully. 'Okay, Sky.'

Skyler invites his friends over and at first Teagan stays in her room with a chair under the doorknob, but after a few hours when they haven't come looking, she slips into the kitchen, starving. Through the open window she sees them in their circle of plastic chairs, one leaning forward to show the dog a slice of pizza.

'C'mon, bitch,' he calls, and Killer stands on her hind legs, revealing her oyster-coloured stomach and its twin rows of thick, pink nipples. Zeb swings the slice back and forth like a pocket watch and the dog's eyes follow it, then he folds it up and stuffs it in his mouth. 'Too slow,' he mumbles, and the others laugh like drains.

'Hey, hey,' Teagan's brother booms, stretching to reach something on the ground. 'Can't ya see she's gagging for it?'

He lifts up an old black planter and they all watch as he tips his beer into it, then pushes it over to Killer with his foot. 'Drink up!' he commands, and the dog ladles up the suds. The four boys cheer.

The next morning, while Skyler is still asleep, Teagan slides behind her bed so he can't see her from the doorway and phones their father. He has her number, of course he does, but he answers as if he doesn't: 'You've reached John.'

'Dad, it's me.'

There is fumbling. 'Teagan,' he says. 'How are you, sweetheart?'

'I'm good.' Her pitch rises uncontrollably, like a released balloon. 'Did Skyler tell you he got a dog?'

The house Teagan and Skyler live in still belongs to their father, though he hasn't lived there in years. It was a useful property back when John was single and working for himself, buying wrecks out of the *Quokka* and fixing them up, but then he found a job at a suburban garage and started going out with his boss's middle-aged daughter, Pippa. Now it makes more sense to stay at her place and not drive all the way down from the hills, and Pippa would never live at John's, anyway; it's too out of date, too far from everything. Pippa's father is thinking of retiring and selling his almost-son-in-law the business, and for that John needs to demonstrate commitment. Life with Pippa keeps John very busy.

'A dog,' he repeats. Teagan hears the sweep of fabric as he rubs the phone against his shirt. 'What kind?'

'I don't know.' Teagan didn't plan this part of the conversation. She tries to picture Killer: the dark coat fading to silver along her flanks; her square face and dropped ears; the tight tail held close to her rump. 'A big one?'

'Like what?' Her father sounds irritated. 'A Great Dane? A Husky? A German Shepherd?'

Teagan knows very little about dogs. They once had a bitsa called So-So who liked to chase, jumping hard on his prey when he caught it. Once, when she was four, that dog hunted her down the passageway, landed on her back with all four paws, and hooked a tooth into the base of her skull. The gash bled warm and heavy through her hair and down the back of her shirt. She went to tell her mother, who was lying on the couch, a towel over her eyes. 'So-So bit me,' Teagan said, and her mother pulled herself to an elbow and lifted the compress from her face. The child stood intact before her, pink arms at her sides, nose scraped where the dog had forced her into the carpet. 'You're fine,' she groaned, and Teagan turned away obediently, revealing the waterfall of purple blood. She'd needed six stitches to close the hole, and now when she lifts her ponytail the white line is still there, a rectangle of hair missing where the doctor had to shave it away.

'I'm really not sure,' Teagan says to John. 'She's just a big black dog.'

John blows noisily down the phone. Metal clangs in the background, followed by voices.

'Sorry, are you at work?'

'It's eight o'clock in the morning, Teagan,' he says, drolly. 'Why aren't *you* at work?'

'My shift isn't till eleven.'

'Have you asked them again about going full-time?'

Teagan has not. Her manager at the supermarket is frightening, spiteful. 'I don't think they have the hours.'

'Well, you need to ask.'

'Okay.'

'Look,' her father says definitively, 'it's fine about the dog. The place could do with some protection. There's some engines lying around that are still worth money.'

'Okay,' Teagan repeats. A sense of doom rolls through her. 'Just wanted you to know.'

'Thanks for telling me.' There's a final rustle and then the line clears. Her father speaks directly in her ear. 'Good girl.'

*

The next day she takes a basket of washing to hang on the line, stopping halfway across the lawn when she sees the dog. Killer sits patiently in the sun, head lifted like a precocious student. She doesn't bark or growl. The plastic pot Skyler filled with beer is discarded a few feet away, dry and ringed with dust.

Teagan puts the basket down and refills the pot from the hose. Remembering how her brother levered the beer towards the dog, she places it on the ground and uses a corner of the washing basket to do the same. Halfway across, the vessel collides with a tuft of grass and tips sideways, sloshing water out. 'Sorry,' she says, and Killer watches passively, her tail flat. Teagan returns to the patio for the outdoor broom, a finer tool, and propels it the rest of the way.

As soon as Teagan withdraws the broom Killer descends, gulping the water down, her pounding tail lifting clouds of sand from the lawn. She finishes and looks up, foamy saliva coursing down her neck. 'More?' Teagan asks, and the tail thumps harder. Teagan hooks the brush-head around the bowl to get it back, filling it higher this time. Again, the dog crouches low to the ground, her chin at the surface of the water, tongue hauling it up like buckets from a well. When it empties again Teagan gets more. She smiles at Killer, who is not such a scary dog this way, frothy and grateful, slack with relief.

'Whatcha doin'?'

Teagan jumps. Her brother has come up behind her, his hair flat from sleep, the collar of his T-shirt slack and yellow. Old alcohol and body odour waft from him as he captures her lightly around the neck.

'Just giving her a drink,' Teagan says, trying not to react. 'She was thirsty.'

Skyler releases her when she's off-balance and she falls on a knee in the dirt. The dog, her third bowl finished, licks her lips. 'I'm tryna train her to be a fucken guard dog.'

'How do you do that?' Teagan asks. Skyler is always better when you make him feel smarter than you are.

He snorts proudly. 'Starvation and thirst, *der*. Make her ravenous. She'll bite anyone that tries to get in.'

'How does thirst work, though? Won't that make her weak?' Teagan makes her eyes wondrous. The dog does the same.

'Makes her angrier.' Skyler shakes his head and inserts a flat hand into the top of his boxer shorts, then pulls back and wipes his fingers on his shirt. 'Okay, fine, give her water. But don't fucken feed her, alright? Don't mess with my training.'

She nods supportively. 'That's a good idea, Sky.'

Skyler looks down at the broom and laughs. His hot nicotine breath settles on Teagan. 'You're scared of her, eh.'

'She's a guard dog.' Teagan looks at Killer sitting under the clothesline, her muzzle damp and shining. Her tail twitches. 'I thought she was meant to be scary.'

Skyler smiles slowly. 'She is,' he says. 'She's gunna be a killer.'

*

Mostly when Teagan isn't at work she stays in her room, not wanting to inadvertently upset her brother; to draw his muttered insults or the threat of his long-nailed hand, flying out to swat between her legs or pinch her hard on the chest. He has spread through the house like an army requisitioning property, like bacteria: the television room, the meals area, the family bathroom, and the sour-smelling toilet off the laundry, its base caked in dust and moist yellow circles, the scrubbing brush broken in its stand. Instead, Teagan goes up the passageway to her father's ensuite, which she was forbidden to use as a child and still treats like a divine place, pushing the brush into the bowl when she's finished, wiping down the sink to leave no trace. To go in and out she passes through the master bedroom with its heavy curtains always drawn, the same claret-coloured bedding from when her mother was around. Teagan would never dare sleep in here, but her brother's friends sometimes do. As soon as they've gone she pulls the grubby sheets away from the mattress, shoves the vacuum cleaner through the carpet, and sluices the ensuite, tears in her eyes from the bleach and the shame. The boys get sick in here from their beer and pot and junk food, do sloppy shits, piss on the seat. Violate her parents' space.

Once a month or so Teagan and Skyler drive into town to have dinner with their father and Pippa at her neat little house. They order Thai and eat out in the courtyard. 'This is better, isn't it?' Pippa says each time, as if she'd considered the other options before making the choice. 'Going out is such a hassle, anyway.' She has children of her own – two girls, Emma and Alexandra – but the visits never overlap. Emma lives in Sydney, where she studies acting, and Alexandra is a lawyer whose time is precious.

Whenever they leave these dinners Teagan has the acute sense of her life being dirty and pointless. Her father and Pippa never say anything, but Teagan looks at the beautiful objects in their home and feels it. Pippa has framed pictures hung on every wall: bright beaches at sunrise, or professional shots of the girls. In the entryway are Emma's headshots, and in the laundry is a sketch of a naked woman – not one of the daughters – with a loose sheet covering her breast and the other on lazy display. In the dining area there's a floating shelf with white wooden letters urging them to LIVE EACH DAY, a sentiment that piques Teagan's despair. She is not living each day. She graduated three years ago but is still at the supermarket where she started working afternoons after school, overseeing the self-checkouts with the terrifying Joanna watching from the cigarette counter. She didn't have the marks to get into uni, which was okay because she didn't know what to study; she meant to do a receptionist course at TAFE, but never ended up enrolling because Joanna asked her to work that day. Since then her hours have dropped: Joanna plays favourites, and Teagan is not one of them.

She knows that if she moved out she'd be happier. She could keep her new place like Pippa's, with unused candles on bookshelves and coffee tables cleared of detritus. But the familiarity and comfort of the house in the hills holds her down like So-So. When she adjusts the crimson coverlet in the big bedroom she can smell her mother's hand cream.

She drifts into the kitchen a few times a day so she can watch Killer through the window. The dog lies on the grass, chin on her front paws, and looks up when Teagan appears. The two of them gaze at each other reverently. 'Hey, girl,' Teagan murmurs. 'Good girl.'

She takes the water out when she knows Skyler isn't home, even though he'd decided to allow it. While she doesn't really fear the dog, she still slides the bowl over with the head of the broom. She didn't fear So-So, either.

Sometimes she sees Skyler outside with Killer, doing their training. He duct-tapes a pillow round his arm and swats it against the dog's muzzle until she shies away. 'Latch! Latch!' he shouts, like a mother frustrated by a squalling baby. He balances on one leg and kicks at the dog's chest only for her to growl and step back. Later, angry, he sits back with a tub of old toy cars and ditches them at the dome of her skull, sneering when she yelps. He won't walk her and she has to defecate in the radius of the clothesline, but she does get fed a little bit: biscuit dust from the ends of packages, crumbs of potato chips, lettuce that slides out of burgers. Like she's a rubbish bin. At night he cooks himself steak or chops on the barbecue, smirking as Killer becomes frantic over the smell. When it's done he uses tongs to dangle the meat in front of her, the way Zeb taunted her with the pizza. Watching Killer open her mouth and strain makes Teagan feel as if she's choking. 'You get this when you bite someone,' Skyler tells the dog around mouthfuls of the cooked flesh, grease sliding down his chin. He wipes his slick hands on his thighs and drops the bones out of reach, and a deep hunger swells in Teagan. 'Bitch.'

After her shift at the supermarket Teagan buys a couple of cans of home-brand dog food, smuggling them into the house as if Skyler will pounce. He isn't even home. Pulling open the side door, she sees the dog lying belly-up on the ground, her paws bent, legs spread. Teagan goes cold with horror and stumbles onto the lawn. 'Hey! Hey!'

Killer rolls over and lurches upright, alive but weak. She's much skinnier than when Skyler first brought her home, the bones of her shoulders and ribs stark corrugations beneath her coat. Her muzzle has narrowed and the loose skin hangs over her teeth. The old pot is empty, so Teagan fills that first, forgetting herself and putting it down by Killer with a bare hand.

Teagan goes back to get the dog food from where she dropped it on the patio, then imagines her brother smelling it on Killer's breath or spotting brown flecks in her whiskers. He'd know; he would kill her. Stomach grinding, she takes the cans back to her room, rolling them far under her bed so that they knock against the skirting board. In the kitchen she searches for scraps, the kinds of things Skyler himself would let Killer have, but with a bit more heft: half a tray of cooked lasagne, a bruised apple, three slices of bread, a bag of green grapes. She goes to the front door to be sure her brother's car isn't turning off the road, then returns to Killer, who's finished her water. Teagan sits in front of the dog cross-legged and puts the items on the dying grass between them. 'Here, Cassie,' she whispers. 'Eat up.'

*

Skyler's hand slides along the top of the couch while they're watching television and Teagan tenses as his fingers jab upwards, disappearing into the spout of her ponytail. 'Hold still,' he orders. There's a feathery touch along the back of her neck and her stomach seizes at the idea of a fat black cockroach, the movement caught by her brother, who doesn't fear bugs the way she does. She's about to beg him to get it off, to take it outside for Killer to devour the sticky proteins, then realises the sensation is just the raw ends of his fingers as they move away from her hairline.

'What are you *doing*?' She tries to sound annoyed and not repulsed.

He skates his nails up and down the knobs at the top of her spine. 'Your scar,' he says finally. 'You can still see it.'

'I know,' she says, twisting away.

At last Skyler's fingers drops back, though his arm is still stretched past her shoulders, as if they're on a date. 'You made them put So-So down,' he says.

This is a refrain that began after the dog was destroyed; Teagan thought Skyler had forgotten, moved on to other taunts. 'I didn't tell them to.'

'You made So-So chase you.'

Teagan doesn't know why the dog tracked her down the passage that day. She remembers believing, years ago, that her brother had rubbed cooked mince into her hair, but she no longer thinks that's possible. Their parents would've smelled it, or the doctors who stitched her up. It's too extreme a violation, even for Skyler.

'I was four,' Teagan argues.

'I loved that dog.' True only because Skyler says it.

Teagan lifts her legs to her chest and hunches forward so his forearm can't brush her skin. This is an old script they're following, and she no longer knows her lines.

'You gunna try and get Killer put down, too?' Skyler asks.

'No.' She answers as quickly as possible. 'What makes you think that?'

'You don't like her.'

'Yes, I do.'

'She's a dangerous dog.'

Teagan is careful not to deny that, because Skyler will take it as a rejection of his intermittent 'training'. 'Only to intruders,' she says.

'What if she thinks you're an intruder?'

'She's too smart.'

A smile creeps across Skyler's face like the cockroach Teagan felt moving up her neck. 'I got a good deal, eh.'

Eventually, Skyler's arm falls back off the couch. Twenty minutes after that, Teagan can leave.

*

Killer seems to like grapes best so Teagan buys them specially, waiting until Skyler drives off before taking them outside. Killer has perked up a little with Teagan's attention, but she's still in a bad way. Her tail is a spring that twangs when she sees Teagan approach. There's a chemical smell that worries her, and dark brown patches of urine on the ground.

'Hey, girl,' she murmurs. 'I've got a treat for you.'

One by one Teagan rolls the small white globes across to Killer, who snaps them half-heartedly out of the dirt. 'Good girl.' The words are so soft she isn't sure she's said them. 'What a good girl you are. What a good girl.'

That night Teagan is going to the toilet when she passes Skyler at the table, smoking, staring out into the backyard. She feels sick at the sight of him but Skyler demands acknowledgment. 'What's up?'

'That dog's a fucken waste of my time,' he grumbles. Phlegm oscillates in his throat.

'What's wrong?'

'Zeb came round and the fucken bitch didn't even bark.'

'She's met Zeb, though.'

'She's spose'ta be mean.'

Teagan tries to sound unattached. 'Maybe you should give her back.'

Skyler's cigarette smoulders. He doesn't respond.

'I mean, if she's not doing the job.' Emotion swells in Teagan's throat and for a second she's afraid she'll laugh. 'Make the guy take her back.'

'You can't fool me,' her brother says flatly.

Fear makes Teagan stand up straight. She looks past Skyler and sees the black mound of the dog beneath the clothesline, not moving. 'What?'

'You're scared of Killer. Y'want me to get rid of her.'

She scratches a mosquito bite, trying to be cautious. 'I am a bit scared. She's an intimidating dog.'

'She's useless,' Skyler spits.

'Because she didn't bark at Zeb?'

'She should've gone bat-shit at the chain. Tried to rip his throat off.'

'Zeb's a fucking dog himself, Sky,' Teagan blurts. It feels good to say it. She remembers Zeb's long nose sliding around her door. His sharp, stained teeth; the spittle on his jaw. 'She probably recognised her own kind.'

Her brother laughs in disbelief. 'The bitch comes out,' he says admiringly. 'So you reckon I should keep the dog?'

'Or what?' Her heart leaps. 'Give her back?'

'No.' Skyler suckles at the cigarette. 'Put her down. Get a rifle and stick it in her ear.'

'Keep the dog,' she says coolly. 'She'll come good. Just wait.'

With a grumble of assent, Skyler turns back towards the yard.

Teagan walks slowly up the passage to her father's ensuite and locks the door behind her. She bends over the toilet bowl, seeing her shaky form in the water. Tomorrow, when Skyler's gone, she'll give the dog both cans of food, then get the bolt cutters and set her free.

*

Her father phones early, while Teagan is still in bed. 'I'm at the gate,' he says, without greeting her. 'Let me in, would you?'

Teagan is in a shirt and underwear, and she steps into her work pants before going outside. Her father hasn't been to the house for months, and she wonders if he's fought with Pippa or one of the girls. He seems to get along with Alexandra and Emma, but Pippa would side with her daughters over John in an instant if she had to. If the situation were reversed, though, her father wouldn't do the same. He'd pick his girlfriend every day of the week.

She goes to the front of the property and unlocks the gate. John stands with his arms crossed hard into his stomach, his ute parked at an angle behind him. Skyler's car isn't there. 'Is everything okay?'

'I want to get a look at this dog,' John says, stepping through. He wears pressed pants and a button-down shirt, stylish sunglasses hanging from the collar. 'Ken next door rang to say he's worried.'

Teagan hurries to close the padlock and follow him up the driveway. 'She's not vicious or anything.' She wants to tuck an arm into her father's and lean in deep, letting him take up her weight. She checks behind them to see if Skyler's coming.

'Where is she?'

'Out the back.'

As they round the side of the house Teagan expects the animal to be emaciated and depressed but still able to sit up, her eyes fixed on the two figures. Her tail will tremble and John, seeing her condition, will announce that they got there just in time. *This dog needs to eat,* he'll say, rubbing the shale plains of Killer's haunches, the dog closing her eyes in ecstasy. Teagan will get the dog food and bring the feast out onto the lawn. As she works the can opener Killer will lean in, quivering, and give Teagan a long, gentle lick up the wrist. *She likes you, look*, John will say. *You're clearly the only one she trusts.*

Killer is stretched out at the bottom of the clothesline, her stomach against the square of anchoring cement, legs splayed in front and behind her. Her tongue has slipped out of her slackened mouth and her bony hips quiver against the earth.

'Jesus Christ,' John says. He crouches, careful not to get the knees of his pants dirty, and takes Killer by the jaw. Teagan wants to shout for him to watch out, that Skyler's been training her to attack, but the dog's head just lolls over, tipping the desiccated tongue the other way. A groan shudders through her. 'Haven't you been giving her water?'

Tears line the bottoms of Teagan's eyes. The pot is in the grass nearby, still a third full, some sand pooling at the bottom. 'She's got water, look.'

'What's he been feeding her?'

Nothing, Teagan wants to say. 'All kinds of stuff.'

John has pulled the water over and is trying to guide Killer's snout into the bowl. 'Bread. Leftovers. Grapes.'

John looks Killer over. 'Grapes?'

'Yeah,' Teagan says, feeling uncertain. She stares at her feet on the grass. 'She likes them.'

'Grapes are toxic to dogs. Does he know that?'

Teagan feels cold. She tucks her hands into the burn of her armpits. 'What?'

'It messes up their kidneys.'

Her father slides a hand under the dog's chest and tucks another behind her withered thighs, and Teagan realises he's trying to pick her up. She steps forward to help but John has got his footing, the dog's legs dangling between his arms like cables. Killer doesn't make a sound.

'Has he been torturing her on purpose?'

'No!'

Shaking his head, John heads back towards the road. The dog's four bundled paws bounce lifelessly with each step. Teagan tries to keep up.

'He was training her to be a guard dog, Dad. She just likes grapes.'

'Well, they're poison.' Her father's powerful strides push him away from her. He shouts over his shoulder. 'I'm taking her to a vet.'

'Do you want me to come?' she asks, fumbling to unlock the gate. 'I can tell them what happened.'

'What do you think they're going to do, Teagan?'

She holds the top of the gate and leans into it, crying. John opens the back door of his car and eases the dog onto the seat.

'Ken said the dog was being starved. I told him you wouldn't let that happen.' John slams the door. 'Good thing he insisted.'

He pulls out onto the road in a blur of dust. The day is warming up but Teagan stays pressed to the gate like a prisoner, the hot metal marking her flesh. In the heat, her mouth dries out. Her straining thighs shake.

Soon Skyler will rise from wherever he spent last night, wipe dried saliva from his chin, and get into his car. Back home he'll go out to check on the dog. *You bitch! Where the fuck is she?*

Teagan practises, speaking carefully with her fat, dry tongue. The sun stings her scar. *I woke up and she was gone.* She feels the presence at her back, gaining on her. *Must've slipped her harness. Or maybe that guy stole her back.* A rumble as the predator launches. *I let her go, Sky. I couldn't take it anymore.* Sharpness penetrates the soft spot at the base of her skull, peeling her open like a tin of dog food.

There's a hum in the air, getting louder. Her brother's car turns into the driveway.

Previous Publications

'Killer' was shortlisted for the Bridport Short Story Prize 2019

'The Spaniel' was commended in the *Griffith Review* Novella Project IV.

'Bella' was published in the *Newcastle Short Story Award Anthology 2019*

Acknowledgements

Brooke Dunnell is runner up in the 2020 Carmel Bird Digital Literary Award for *Female(s and) Dogs* along with Katerina Cosgrove for *Zorba The Buddha*. The winner is Michalia Arathimos for *Apologia*. The judge of the 2020 award was Justin Wolfers.

This award is named in honour of renowned Australian author Carmel Bird, who has published a range of short fiction, novels and books on writing and was awarded the Patrick White Award for Literature in 2016.

Launched in 2017, the Carmel Bird Digital Literary Award is an annual competition that showcases new works of short fiction up to 30,000 words in length from Australian writers. It is run by Spineless Wonders and supported by the Copyright Agency's Cultural Fund.

Finalists in the Carmel Bird Digital Literary Award are published electronically by Spineless Wonders.

www.shortaustralianstories.com.au

Biography

Brooke Dunnell is a Perth writer whose short fiction has been published in *Best Australian Stories*, *Meanjin*, Westerly and other journals and anthologies. Her work has been recognised in a range of competitions including the Neilma Sidney Short Story Prize 2017 and the Bridport Short Story Prize 2019. She won the 2021 Fogarty Literary Award.

About This Series

Female(s And) Dogs by Brooke Dunnell is published as part of the Spineless Wonders Smalls series of small format paperbacks released to celebrate our tenth year in publishing.

To find out about other books published in this series, go to www.shortaustralianstories.com.au

www.shortaustralianstories.com.au